"Jaime, you don't know what you're tangling with...."

"Is that why you came here tonight?" Jaime demanded bitterly. "To persuade me to leave the committee?"

"You'll put your own crazy interpretation on my actions. You always did," Blake said bitterly. "Just remember that it isn't just yourself you're risking, it's my daughter as well, and as long as you're still my wife...."

"Then I'll just have to make sure I'm not your wife for much longer, won't I?"

"You seem to have forgotten that for a divorce you need either my agreement or proof that we haven't cohabited for over two years.... You have neither."

She could have wept. Not ten minutes ago they had been as close as two human beings could be. Now it was all gone. A lesson to her for having mistaken desire for love.

Books by Penny Jordan

HARLEQUIN PRESENTS

These books may be available at your local bookseller.

Don't miss any of our special offers. Write to us at the following address for information on our newest releases.

Harlequin Reader Service
P.O. Box 52040, Phoenix, AZ   85072-2040
Canadian address: P.O. Box 2800, Postal Station A,
5170 Yonge St., Willowdale, Ont.   M2N 6J3

PENNY JORDAN

campaign for loving

Harlequin Books

TORONTO • NEW YORK • LONDON
AMSTERDAM • PARIS • SYDNEY • HAMBURG
STOCKHOLM • ATHENS • TOKYO • MILAN

Harlequin Presents first edition February 1985
ISBN 0-373-10761-7

Original hardcover edition published in 1984
by Mills & Boon Limited

Printed in U.S.A.

CHAPTER ONE

As she unlocked the door of her Mini, Jaime glanced quickly at her watch, expelling a faint sigh of relief. Three o'clock. She still had plenty of time to pick up her three-year old-daughter, Fern, from playschool.

At first, when her mother had suggested she move back to Dorset, she had been dubious. She and Blake had lived in London during the brief eighteen months of their marriage and she had been reluctant to move away. Now she could acknowledge that her reluctance had stemmed from her hope that Blake would come looking for her and beg her to go back to him. For a girl of twenty-three she had been extremely naive, she thought sardonically. The unflattering alacrity with which Blake had accepted the challenge she had flung at him in the heat of her tempestuous outburst ought to have warned her, but it hadn't. It had taken Suzy Monteith to do that. Suzy had worked with Blake on the *Globe*'s Foreign Affairs team for several years and Blake had never made any secret of the fact that they had at one time been lovers. Suzy had never liked her Jaime realised with the benefit of hindsight, and no doubt she had thoroughly enjoyed telling her of her husband's request to his editor that he be sent abroad to cover the war in El Salvador, only twenty-four hours after she had accused him of putting his job before his marriage, more or less giving him an ultimatum to choose between her and working for the *Globe*.

Suzy had called round on the pretext of inviting them both to a party she was giving. But Jaime hadn't even waited for Blake to come home that evening, she had simply packed her things and gone round to a friend's flat where she had stayed for two weeks, willing Blake to appear and beg her to come back to him.

Of course he hadn't done and by then she had known that the possibility that she might be pregnant was a certainty. She had written to him then, an angry bitter letter to which he didn't reply, making it obvious that he didn't want her or their child—she had offered him a choice and he had made one—excluding her completely from his life. Her pregnancy had wrapped her in an anaesthetising shawl which numbed all pain. Blake's letters she returned unopened, accepting her mother's suggestion that she return home simply because she had no means of supporting herself, and was was determined not to accept any money from Blake. He hadn't wanted a child—he had made that more than clear to her. His lifestyle could barely accommodate a wife, never mind the responsibility of children, and that had been another subject for contention between them.

The truth was that they should never have married, Jaime thought as she manoeuvred her car down the bumpy lane that led from the old school hall she used for her dance and exercise studio to the village. And it was her fault that they had married. All Blake had wanted was an affair—but she had been naive and very much in love. When he discovered that she was still a virgin he had given in to the subtle pressure she had put on him and, within six months of meeting, they had been married.

Right from the start she had known that she wasn't really equipped to enter Blake's world. Shy and rather retiring by nature, she had gone to London at the urgings of a schoolfriend and her mother, and although she quite enjoyed her job as a secretary in a busy advertising agency, she had never really lost her longing for the peace and relative simplicity of the village she had grown up in. She had met Blake at a party, flattered and slightly bemused that he should single her out for attention. She knew she wasn't exactly unattractive but she had lived in London long enough by then to realise that London males expected more than a heart-shaped face, deep blue eyes, black hair and a willow-slim body. They wanted women who could converse with them on their own level, sharp witty women who didn't blush and fumble awkwardly; women who were as sophisticated and worldly as they were themselves.

She had recognised Blake instantly from a current affairs television programme he had participated in, but the effect of his lean, sun-tanned features and his air of cool cynicism were far more devastating in real life than they were on the television screen. She had had the impression that his green eyes were laughing at her, but when, seconds later, they roved her body with a sensual appraisal that was almost a physical caress, she hadn't been able to hide her response from him. Blake! Even now, just thinking about him made her pulses race and her mouth go dry. He had been, at first, a patient and then a very passionate lover, drawing her out of her shell of shy reserve, teaching her to please him and find joy in her own pleasure. As befitted a man who lived on the edge of danger, he brought excitement and challenge into her life, but she was constantly worried that she would never be enough for him; that after a while her inability to meet him as an equal would lead him to grow bored with her. Before their marriage he had dated sophisticated, glamorous women, and Jaime had always secretly compared herself to them and found herself wanting. If she hadn't blurted out to him that she loved him and that he would be her first lover, would he still have wanted to marry her?

'He married you because that was the only way he could get you into bed,' Suzy had told her tauntingly, 'but you'll never keep him—he's bored already. You see, Blake's like that. When he wants something, he goes after it single-mindedly, that's what makes him such a good reporter. He wanted *you* because you were a challenge. . . .'

And she, instead of trying to understand him, had begged him to give up his job and find another one that would mean less travel. That had been the cause of their final row. . . . Perhaps, because her own father had died when she was so young, she had always cherished in her mind a clear picture of what she wanted her life to be, and that picture contained herself, her husband and their two children, living cosily in a village very like the one she had been brought up in; a safe, secure little world, a universe away from Blake's lifestyle.

People thought she had got over him and her marriage to him. She talked openly to Fern about her father; she answered whatever questions people asked her, but only she knew the truth. She still loved Blake as desperately now as she had done the day she left him. But at least in the intervening four years she had achieved some maturity, she reflected as she brought her Mini to a halt outside the playschool building. At least she had finally accepted that Blake had the right to make his own decisions about his career and his life, but that didn't stop her regretting her folly in leaving him. If she had stayed, perhaps they could have worked something out . . . perhaps. . . . Angrily, she dragged her mind away from the past. Blake had made it more than clear how much he regretted their marriage. He had never even asked to see Fern. He hadn't wanted a child and, although he had offered to support them financially, he had made no attempt to get to know his daughter.

Charles had told her she ought to get a divorce. She had known Charles Thomson since her schooldays, and she knew, without any conceit, that he would marry her tomorrow if she gave him any encouragement. It was ironic that Charles was tailormade to fit her childhood image of the perfect husband and father, but he was as exciting as cold rice pudding, and her body, which had been awakened and tutored by Blake's, instinctively repudiated him as a lover.

She knew why she had never bothered to get a divorce. She had no wish to marry again, but what about Blake? Was it just that he had never had the time between assignments to bring their marriage to a formal end, or was it simply that, having married once, he had no intention of repeating his mistake? Unlike her, Blake did not seem to lack congenial companions of the opposite sex. Over the years, she had seen him featured in several newspaper photographs as the escort of glamorous women.

'Mummy . . . Mummy. . . .'

The impatient and reproving voice of her daughter checked her thoughts. Fern was all Blake's child. She had her father's unruly, dark brown hair and his green eyes. And her personality held echoes of Blake's as well. A pragmatic, intelligent child, she sometimes gave Jaime the uncomfortable feeling that their roles were reversed and that she was the child. She even seemed to accept her own lack of a father. She had seen his photograph and knew that he lived and worked in London, but seemed to accept that his life lay apart from theirs.

'. . . and Mrs Childs told us a story. . . but I

knew it wasn't real. Frogs can't turn into princes, not really. . . .'

Jaime glanced into her daughter's scornful green eyes and sighed. She herself had been at least ten before she had finally and reluctantly abandoned fairy stories.

'You're daydreaming again . . .' the small firm voice accused. 'Granny says you've always got your head up in the clouds. . . .'

When Jaime repeated this comment to her mother later in the evening when Fern was in bed, Sarah Cummings laughed. Married at eighteen, a mother at nineteen, she was, in Jaime's view, far too young-looking and vigorous to be anyone's grandmother. A partner in a thriving antique business in the local market town her mother had the knack of drawing people to her, Jaime reflected watching her. Her once fair hair was tinged with grey now, but she still had the same youthful figure she had always had, and she still seemed to radiate that special sort of energy that Jaime always associated with her.

'Fern's like me,' her mother commented pragmatically, 'a down-to-earth Taurean. . . .'

'Umm, I was thinking today how like Blake she is. . . .'

'Don't tell me you're worrying about her lack of father again,' Sarah said drily, correctly interpreting her remark. 'Well, if you're thinking of marrying Charles to provide her with one, I shouldn't bother. She's already running rings round him.'

That Charles found it difficult to talk to her

young daughter Jaime already knew. An only child himself, he was always uneasy in Fern's presence and she seemed to know it and take advantage of his awkwardness.

'You're not worrying about the studio, are you?' Sara asked her daughter, noticing the frown pleating her fair skin. 'I thought it was just about beginning to pay its way.'

'Yes, it is.' At first on her return to her home Jaime had been wholly dependent on her mother, but once Fern had started playschool, she had trained in exercise and dance, and then, when she was qualified, she had opened her own school which was beginning to get an excellent reputation locally. She was fortunate in being able to rent a now-empty school hall at a very reasonable cost, and the knowledge that she had achieved something for herself through her effort and skill had boosted her self-confidence. Because she always looked so calm and self-possessed, few people guessed at the deep sense of inadequacy she suffered from. Indeed, it was only since she had left Blake that she had come to terms with it herself.

'So, what's worrying you?' her mother probed.

'Charles came to see me today. He's heard that Caroline means to sell the Abbey to a property developer and that it's going to be knocked down and a housing estate built.'

'Mmm . . . I shouldn't think she'll be able to go ahead with the sale. The Abbey is a listed building, you know.'

'And Caroline can be very determined.'

Jaime had gone to school with Caroline Travers, although they had never been good friends. Caroline's father had made a fortune in industry and had bought the Abbey and retired there. Caroline had inherited quite a substantial sum from him on his death, but she was a lady with very expensive tastes and she had never liked the Abbey.

'Charles wants me to go round and have a word with her—try to persuade her to reconsider. . . .'

'Why doesn't he go himself?' Sarah asked forthrightly. 'Really, the man is a fool. I honestly believe he's terrified that Caroline would seduce him.'

Jaime grinned at her mother's percipience. 'He did say that he thought the initial approach would be better coming from me—a "woman to woman appeal",' Jaime quoted.

'"Woman to man eater" doesn't he mean?' her mother quipped. 'Really, Charles is impossible. I don't know why you bother with him.'

'Because he's an old friend and he's my solicitor. . . .'

'And he's also a very safe wall to hide behind. Jaime, you're twenty-six, and a very attractive woman, but you behave as though you've voluntarily gone into purdah. . . .'

'You were even younger when you were widowed. . . .'

'Yes, but I didn't eschew all male company because of it. . . .'

'But you've never remarried.'

'No, because I preferred being single. You

don't. You need marriage, Jaime, I never did. I was too independent to commit myself to the sort of relationship marriage was in my day. I loved your father and I missed him terribly, but I didn't live like a nun the way you do. Blake. . . .'

'I don't want to talk about him. . . .'

Jaime turned away, hoping that her face wouldn't betray her. Her mother didn't know that she still loved Blake, and every time she mentioned him, Jaime retreated from the conversation like a flower curling protectively back on itself. Her mother had liked Blake. They had got on well together, chatting with an ease that had left her envious when she heard Blake's deep laughter mingling with her mother's. She had been jealous of the ease with which they became at home with one another, just as she had been jealous of anyone who got close to her husband. It was no wonder he had lost his temper with her, she reflected as she went into the kitchen on the pretext of wanting a drink. When she thought about it, it was a miracle he had stayed with her so long as he had. No man likes jealous scenes, and on occasions she had behaved like a spoiled child, demanding more and more of his time and attention because of her deep-rooted insecurity, her inability to believe that he loved and needed her with the same intensity with which she loved and needed him. She had created an atmosphere which must have been claustrophobic, driving him away from her in her frantic attempts to keep him with her. No one would ever know how much she regretted her behaviour, or how much she longed for a second chance, she thought as she reached automatically for the coffee. Her mother thought the subject of Blake was taboo because she hated him. That was what she had claimed when she first came home, driven to say so because she couldn't admit the truth, and she had never corrected that misconception.

When Charles commiserated with her about her marriage she had to grit her teeth to stop herself from telling him the truth—that the faults were all on her side. There had hardly been a night in the three years since Fern's birth when she hadn't longed for Blake's presence, and yet she couldn't regret Fern who had, in her way, been the reason for that final argument. Knowing that she might be pregnant, and that her pregnancy had been the result of her deliberate carelessness, she had panicked when Blake had declared quite firmly that he didn't want children. But what was the use of raking over the past?

'Perhaps you're right,' she said to her mother when she carried the coffee tray back into the small sitting room. 'Perhaps I ought to tell Charles to start divorce proceedings.'

Because she was bending over the tray, she missed the brief frown that touched her mother's forehead, and when she looked up it was gone, the older woman's face enviably serene.

'Charles is organising a committee to formally protest against any plans to pull down the Abbey,' Jaime told her mother. 'He wants me to be the secretary.'

'Will you do it?'

'Umm, I think so. It's a beautiful old building.'

'Talking of beautiful old buildings, I've booked my holiday at last. Ten days in Rome, in a month's time.'

'You mean that Henry is actually letting you go on your own?'

Henry Oliver was her mother's partner in the antique business, and had been her faithful admirer for as long as Jaime could remember.

'That's one of the advantages of being independent,' Sarah pointed out with a smile. 'I don't *have* to ask him.'

A week later, carefully noting down the minutes of the meeting Charles had called to discuss ways and means of preventing the Abbey from being destroyed, Jaime pushed a wayward strand of dark curling hair out of her eyes.

'You look about sixteen, poring over that notebook,' an admiring male voice whispered in her ear. 'How about letting me take you out for dinner when this is over?'

'No thanks, Paul.'

Paul Davis was their local celebrity, the Managing Director of their local radio station. He was also married, although he made no attempt to hide his many affairs from his wife.

'Spoilsport.'

Jaime returned her attention to the meeting. Charles was speaking, and she groaned inwardly, knowing his propensity for long and dull speeches. Fern was with Mrs Widdows next door, as Sarah Cummings was also out that evening, and Jaime had promised that she would be back by eight. It was seven now. Paul Davis was also glancing at his watch, and when Charles paused he made full use of the opportunity to stand up and bring the meeting to a rather abrupt halt. Charles looked pained and flustered. 'Rather like an irritated St Bernard,' Jaime thought watching him.

'I hadn't finished speaking,' he complained to Jaime in aggrieved accents later. 'Have you been to see Caroline yet?'

'No, I'll go tomorrow. But she and I were never friends, Charles, and I don't think an approach from me will do the slightest good.'

'Perhaps not, but at least she'd know that we mean to do something. It is a listed building after all. . . .'

Jaime thought of other listed buildings which had become piles of rubble in dubious circumstances, but said nothing—if she didn't leave soon, she'd be late for Fern.

Her route took her past the entrance to the Abbey. As she drove past, a car was turning in at the gates, and she caught a glimpse of a male outline before the car disappeared. One of Caroline's lovers? If so, this man must be rather more wealthy than they usually were. He had been driving a menacing-looking black Ferrari.

'No . . . look, you do it this way. . . .' Fern's clear, high-pitched voice reached her as she knocked on Mrs Widdows' door.

'I was just showing Mrs Widdows how to make a house,' she explained when she saw Jaime. 'A man telephoned after you'd gone out and asked to speak to Granny. He asked me what my name was, and I told him. He was nice.'

It was rare for Fern to make any comment on other adults, but as her mother was out Jamie was unable to question her about the unknown male who had won her daughter's approval.

It was perhaps cowardly of her to take Fern with her the following afternoon when she finally plucked up the courage to go and see Caroline, but Charles had telephoned in the morning, insisting that she go, and having Fern with her gave her something else to worry about other than the coming interview.

Caroline had never liked her; Jaime knew that they were worlds apart for all the similarity in their ages. Caroline had come to her wedding, and she could vividly remember the predatory look in her eyes when she saw Blake. There must be very few women immune to Blake's wholly male, sexual aura. During their brief marriage she had soon come to recognise the look in other women's eyes which said that they were imagining him as their lover. It had driven her into paroxysms of jealous insecurity. How could Blake genuinely prefer her to these sexy, assured women?

As it was a pleasant day she had elected to walk to the Abbey, her decision in no way connected with the fact that walking would delay the inevitable confrontation with Caroline, she taunted herself as she fastened Fern's sandals.

One day her daughter was going to be an extremely attractive woman, and when she was Jaime was determined that she would have far more self-confidence than she had ever had.

'I like this green dress,' Fern told her complacently. 'It's my favourite.'

'It matches your eyes,' Jaime told her. 'Are you ready?'

'Yes, I like your dress too, Mummy.'

It had been a present from her mother the previous year. It was quite simple, white crinkle cotton, with shoe-string straps and an A-line skirt, the ideal dress for a hot, sunny afternoon. Her skin tanned well and the white fabric showed off her smooth golden arms and shoulders. She had taken more care than usual with her make-up and hair. When she looked happy, her eyes glowed like sapphires, Blake had once told her, and he had bought her a sapphire engagement ring to match them. She still had it, but could not wear it because of the memories it brought with it. She felt her heart contract with pain and regret.

Fern was an entertaining companion, chattering away at her side as they headed for the Abbey, Jaime matching her steps to her daughter's slower ones.

'It's a very big house, isn't it?' Fern commented when they turned into the drive, 'but I think I like Granny's cottage best.'

Fern moved with a natural grace Jaime noticed, watching her daughter, unaware that her lithe delicacy had been inherited from her. Jaime had always enjoyed dancing. The discipline of teaching others, of helping them and watching their own appreciation grow with ability gave her an intense feeling of satisfaction. Fern tugged on her hand as she bent to examine a clump of ragged robin, and not for the first time Jaime gave mental thanks for the fact that her daughter had such an equable and sunny temperament. Fern would never suffer as she had done from an excess of sensitivity and over-emotionalism. 'You're too hard on yourself,' her mother always said when she voiced this fact. 'You have many things to recommend yourself, Jaime, you just don't realise it.' It sometimes seemed to Jaime that her mother had been trying to bolster her self-confidence all her life, but she had just never possessed the sturdy independence which characterised both her mother and her daughter.

The Abbey loomed before them, grey and ivy-coloured. Although not a beautiful house, it possessed a mellow air of continuity that had always appealed to Jaime. It had once been an Abbey, although little of the original building remained. It had been rebuilt during the reign of Charles the Second and, although Caroline complained that she found the panelled down-stairs rooms gloomy and depressing, Jaime loved them.

Mrs March, Caroline's housekeeper, answered the door, beaming at Fern, who responded with a happy grin of her own.

'Why don't I take her into the kitchen and give her some of my home-made gingerbread?' she suggested, not realising that she was depriving Jaime of the emotional support she felt she needed. 'Miss Caroline's in the drawing room,' she added.

No doubt Mrs March knew quite well why she was here, Jaime reflected, watching her daughter follow the housekeeper without a backward glance. The panelling had been removed from the drawing room by Caroline's father, but the graceful stucco ceiling remained, and the Adam fireplace added by a Georgian owner. Caroline had completely refurnished the house when she inherited it. Personally, Jaime loathed the cold starkness of the modern Italian furniture she had chosen, but there was no doubt that it made a stunning setting for her startling beauty. Dark red hair framed her face in an aureole of curls, the leather trousers and silk blouse she was wearing being a soft khaki colour which emphasised her colouring. As always, she was immaculately made-up. She had played at modelling when she first left school and had picked up enough tips to achieve what always seemed to Jaime to be an effortlessly glamorous look. She reminded Jaime of the women who had pursued Blake, both before and after their marriage. Brittle, expensive, beautiful predators who lived by their own rules. Women she could never hope to compete with. 'Why bother?' her mother had once said lightly when she had tried to confide her fears to her. Blake had chosen to marry *her*, but she had never been able to rid herself of the conviction that, somehow, she had coerced him into marriage and that had been something she hadn't been able to tell her mother. She had been too deeply ashamed to admit to her that she didn't have the strength to be as independent as Sarah was. She had always felt that, secretly, she must have been a disappointment to her mother; that although she had never shown or expressed any impatience, there must have been some. 'You underestimate yourself too much Jaime.' That was what she had always said, and Jaime would have been surprised if she had known that, far from comparing her with Caroline to her own discredit, most people would have found far more appeal in her own natural beauty and quiet intelligence than in Caroline's showy, pushy manners.

'Well, well if it isn't Miss Goody Two Shoes,' Caroline mocked. The nickname was a throwback to their schooldays, and Jaime managed to hold back the humiliating scald of colour she could feel rising up under her skin.

'No need to ask what you're doing here,' Caroline continued tauntingly. 'But what happened to the cavalry?'

'If you mean Charles, he's had to go to Dorchester to a meeting,' Jaime responded evenly. 'Caroline, surely it can't be true that you intend to sell the Abbey to a developer?'

'Why not?' Caroline asked carelessly, 'After all, it's mine to do with as I choose.' Without inviting Jaime to sit down, she drifted elegantly over to one of the uncomfortable-looking modern chairs, crossing her legs at the ankle, sure of herself as a woman in a way that Jaime felt she could never emulate.

'But it is a listed building,' Jaime reminded her quietly. Caroline shrugged. 'So what. . . . If you feel so strongly about it, you can always put in a more attractive bid. The current one is £250,000.' She laughed unpleasantly at Jaime's expression.

The sound of Fern's excited voice interrupted Jaime's thought flow. She could see her daughter in the garden, walking towards the French windows, chattering animatedly to the man at her side.

Jaime's heart seemed to do a somersault and then stop beating as she stared disbelievingly at the dark head bent towards her daughter's. She started to shake, her sight blurring; the two heads of dark brown hair so similar that they merged into one. Caroline got up and opened the French doors.

'Blake, darling, there you are. I thought you were writing. . . .' There was malice in her eyes as she directed a contemptuous look at Jaime's white face. 'You seem to have given poor Jaime rather a shock, didn't you let her know you were coming?'

As she watched the dark, hawklike profile of her husband turn in her direction, Jaime struggled to retain some composure.

'Jaime and I aren't exactly on intimate terms these days.' The indifferent tone of his voice, the cool aloofness in his green eyes, both combined to increase Jaime's feeling of nausea. She could scarcely believe that this handsome distant man had once possessed her body; had fathered her child.

'I agree.'

'Umm, it seems hard to believe that you were ever that,' Caroline drawled, 'but of course there is Fern.'

Fern! Trying to control the shudders of shocked reaction coursing through her, Jaime looked into her daughter's shining eyes.

'This is my Daddy,' she told Jaime importantly, 'I found him in the garden. He was looking at some flowers. I told him my name and he said that he was my Daddy.'

'Fern, it's time to go home.' How weak and faint her voice sounded. 'Go and say thank you to Mrs Marsh for your gingerbread and then we'll go.'

'I'm sorry about the interruption, Blake,' she heard Caroline apologising as she hurried Fern away. 'It's Mrs Marsh's fault, she should never have let the child loose in the garden.'

Blake's response was an indistinct blur that Jaime didn't stay to hear. Why should she? She already knew how Blake viewed his daughter; in much the same light as he did his wife; as an encumbrance he would prefer to do without.

CHAPTER TWO

'YES, staying up at the Abbey he is . . . writing a book or supposed to be. . . .' The voice faded away as Jaime entered the small post office and her face burned as she recognised who they were talking about. It was as impossible to ignore Blake's presence in the vicinity as it was the sympathetic glances that seemed to follow her everywhere she went these days. Even at the studio she was aware of the faint air of sympathetic concern that surrounded her.

'It's horrible,' she complained to her mother that night. 'I feel as though I'm being treated as the victim of an incurable disease.'

'It's only because people don't want to hurt you,' Sarah sympathised. 'If you talk to them openly about it, they'll soon accept the situation.'

'Why on earth did Blake have to come here?'

'Presumably for the reason Caroline gave you. He needs somewhere to write.'

'Or because he wants to flaunt his affair with Caroline in front of me.'

'Why should he want to do that?' Her mother's glance was calmly shrewd. 'You haven't seen him for four years, and if he wanted to have an affair with Caroline, there's nothing to stop him, although I doubt that she's his type.'

'But why should he need somewhere to

write. . .?' Frustration edged up under her voice, giving it a husky note of impatience.

'Jaime, I know as little about his motives as you do yourself. If you really want answers to all these questions, you must ask him yourself.'

'But to tell Fern that he's her father!' Why must her mother always be so reasonable and fair-minded? Why couldn't she simply side with her without question? Her impartiality was frustrating and, in some strange sense, vaguely threatening.

'He is her father,' Sarah pointed out mildly. 'One of your criticisms of him has always been his lack of interest in her. Try to be consistent, Jaime, my love. What do you want of the man? Or is he just to be a whipping post?'

'I don't believe for one moment that he's come down here simply for Fern's sake.'

'Jaime, I really can't see the point in discussing him with you while you stay in this frame of mind. I can understand why seeing him should shock and even upset you, but for Fern's sake you must try to set aside your own dislike of him, and remember that he *is* her father. Must he be damned for ever, because you quarrelled with him?' she asked quizzically. 'Perhaps he's changed, people do you know,' she said softly. 'Don't rush to meet trouble head on, Jaime. I personally can't believe for one moment that Blake is staying with Caroline simply because he wishes to flaunt any relationship they might have in front of you. He isn't that type of man. Now, I'm going shopping this afternoon. I need to restock my wardrobe for Rome, but I should be back for tea.'

On Wednesday afternoons Jaime closed the studio and usually spent the afternoon with Fern. She had just collected her from playschool and was making a drink when she heard a car stopping outside. Her mother's cottage was the middle one of a row of three with a long front garden and a pleasant, sheltered back one. The kitchen-dining room in which Jaime was standing had windows at either end, and her heart skittered to a standstill as she saw Blake unfold his lean frame from the low-slung black Ferrari she had seen entering the Abbey's drive earlier in the week, and unlock the garden gate.

'Mummy, you're daydreaming again,' Fern criticised sternly. She wanted to run but where was there to run to? And besides, she had left that sort of childish reaction behind her when she left London.

As she opened the door to him, he seemed to tower menacingly over her, dark and forbidding, his jean-clad figure familiar and yet totally alien. He had always affected her in this way; the maleness in him calling out to her deeply feminine core so that her pulse rate quickened and her stomach ached.

'Sensible of you,' he commented when she let him in. His eyes were derisive as he added, 'Knowing you as I do, I half expected to have to break the door down to get in. You always did have a taste for the dramatic.'

'Not to say farcical,' Jaime agreed, watching

the faint surprise replace the derision. 'We do have a back door,' she pointed out, 'and it is open.'

'We have to talk.'

'Do we? I can't think what about.'

'Well, there's Fern for starters.'

'Oh, yes. Of course.' It was her turn to sound derisive. 'Forgive me for not recognising your concern for your daughter straight away, won't you?'

'You know the reason I haven't shown any interest in her before.' His voice was clipped, and if she had not known better she could have imagined there was a trace of angry pain in it.

'What, besides Fern, brings you down here?'

'You heard what Caroline said. I need the peace and quiet to write.'

'A new departure isn't it? You always seemed to manage quite well at the flat.'

'With you for inspiration?' His mouth twisted. 'They were articles, this is a novel—my third to be exact.'

Her heart missed a beat and then hammered painfully. It hurt much more than she could say that there had been such drastic developments in his life and that she had known nothing about them.

'I started the first one just after you left me, after I got back from El Salvador.'

She didn't want to talk about the past. It held far too many unhappy memories. Fern heard their voices and came running out of the kitchen, launching herself at Blake with unabashed enthusiasm. 'Daddy. . . .'

'I'd like to take her out for the afternoon.'

'No ... Wednesday is the only afternoon I have her all to myself.'

'Then come with us.' It was a subtle challenge, reminding her of the many other challenges he had given her in the past and the often childish manner in which she had reacted to them. Fern's smile widened and Jaime knew that if she refused the little girl would be disappointed.

'Very well,' she agreed coolly, suppressing wry amusement as she saw disbelief flicker briefly in Blake's eyes. Had he expected her to refuse? She shrugged aside the thought. What did it matter what he had expected? She wasn't going to leave Fern alone with him, at least not until she knew why he was making this attempt to get to know his daughter. Nor was she going to allow him to provoke her as he had done in the past. With a slight start, she realised she was experiencing none of the tongue-tied anxiety she had previously felt in his presence. Somehow the gulf she had always felt between them seemed to have narrowed, and she no longer stood so much in awe of him. Not that she underestimated him for one moment. Fern was already showing incipient signs of being dazzled by him and her heart ached for her daughter, the pain followed by a fierce wave of protective mother love. Blake would never hurt Fern the way he had hurt her.

'How about the New Forest?' Blake suggested blandly. Jaime bit her lip. They had once spent a weekend there shortly after they were married. Blake had overruled her protests at dinner and, as a consequence, she had drunk rather more wine than was her normal habit. Later, alone together in their room, he had made full use of her intoxicated state to coax from her a physical response to his lovemaking which still held a vivid place in her memories.

'Fine,' she responded lightly. 'Fern will love the ponies.'

He glanced at his watch. 'Well, if we're going to make it there and back in the day, we'd better start out soon.'

He was right, but Jaime suppressed a mental sigh. She had looked forward to a little time on her own from which to draw enough strength to face the prospect of the rest of the afternoon with him.

Fern accepted his presence with her normal placid good sense, although she did comment to Jaime, thankfully while Blake was out of earshot, 'I like my Daddy; he's much nicer than Charles isn't he?'

It didn't take long to get ready. Blake waited for them in the sitting room, commenting admiringly on Fern's new pale pink boilersuit when they rejoined him, although it was on Jaime's slim shape in her faded jeans and soft T-shirt that his eyes lingered.

'I hear you've opened a dance studio,' he remarked, as he opened the front door for them, 'and that it's doing very well.'

'Surprised?' Her voice sounded nastily bitter.

'Why should I be? I always knew you had it in you to make your own way in life, Jaime. That air of helpless desperation is very deceptive. You've made it more than clear to me that you want neither my emotional nor financial support.'

As they were walking down the garden path, Charles' Ford drew up outside, Charles himself emerging from inside it, his eyes going from Jaime to Blake and then back again. Charles had met Blake at the wedding and, as he came towards them, Jaime could almost see the questions hovering on his lips.

'Templeton,' Charles greeted Blake stiffly. 'Quite a surprise.' He looked at Jaime as he spoke, his face taut with disapproval. 'I suppose you're here to discuss the divorce.' His gaze switched back to Blake and Jaime felt her heart lurch precariously. Of course! Stupidly that was something she hadn't thought about. Did Blake want to institute divorce proceedings? If so, he need hardly discuss them with her. They had been separated for longer than the statutory period necessary for an uncontested divorce. 'I'm Jaime's solicitor, and the right thing to do would have been for yours to get in touch with me,' Charles was saying stuffily. 'In fact, your divorce will be quite a simple procedure. . . .'

'Always supposing we want one.' Blake's drawl was calm but something about the way he spoke warned Jaime that he was annoyed. Why? Because Charles had pre-empted him?

'And besides, what makes you think we're discussing divorce? We could be contemplating a reconciliation.'

If she hadn't been so stunned, Jaime might

almost have laughed at Charles's expression. His eyes met hers, but before she could answer the question in them, Blake's hand was on her arm, guiding her towards the car. He opened the door and helped Fern into the back, never once releasing Jaime's arm from his grip.

When he finally put the Ferrari in gear and drove away, Charles was still standing mute, watching them.

'Uncle Charles looked like one of the goldfish at playschool,' Fern commented, watching him, as they drove off. Blake's laughter released Jaime from her stupefied incredulity . . . 'Why did you say that to him?' she demanded angrily. 'Why did you intimate that we might be considering a reconciliation?'

The powerful shoulders shrugged, his profile turning briefly towards her. 'Why not?' he asked blandly. 'It's as likely to be true as his comment about a divorce. At least on my side. Are *you* contemplating divorce proceedings?'

'Are you?'

He made a small, exasperated sound in the back of his throat. 'You know damn well if I was, you'd be the first person to know about them— via me, not some solicitor. The only reason I can think of for divorcing you would be because I wanted to marry someone else. As that doesn't apply, I'm quite happy with the present status quo. Apart from anything else, it acts as a pretty good deterrent.'

'You mean it gives you the freedom to have affairs without giving any commitment,' Jaime commented bitterly.

'It gives you exactly the same freedoms,' Blake pointed out. 'Why was Thomson coming to see you?'

His abrupt change of subject startled her for a moment. For some reason he obviously didn't want to talk about a divorce between them. But then, as he had so cynically commented, he had no reason to divorce her. He had the best of both worlds; the protective status of marriage, and the freedom of a single man.

'Charles? Oh, I expect he wanted to know how I got on at the Abbey.'

'Ah, yes, Caroline waxed most indignant after you'd gone about your plans to stop her selling the place.'

'Not to stop her selling it, it's the fact that she's planning to sell it to a property developer, who will probably pull it down, that we're objecting to.'

'It's a listed building, isn't it?'

'Yes, but when did that stop anyone?'

'You're letting your imagination run away with you. Always a fault of yours. You always did enjoy painting the blackest picture possible.'

They drove some miles in silence before Fern piped up with several questions. Blake answered her with a calm assurance that Jamie found surprising, listening to him tailoring his replies so that the three-year-old would find them easily comprehensible. This was a side of him she had never seen before. Perhaps her mother was right. Perhaps, where Fern was concerned, he had had a change of heart and genuinely wanted to get to know his daughter. How would she be able to cope if Blake came back into her life as Fern's part-time father? She had learned today it was easier to cope with never seeing him than with these brief exchanges, excruciatingly painful after the intimacy she had once shared with him.

With Blake's powerful Ferrari it seemed no time at all before they reached the outskirts of the Forest. Fern laughed excitedly when the powerful car splashed through one of the fords, the jolting throwing Jaime against Blake's hard shoulder. One hand left the wheel as he steadied her, his fingers resting against her body just below the full curve of her breast. She jerked convulsively against his touch as though it burned, watching the mocking arch of his eyebrows.

'Once when you did that it was because you couldn't wait for me to make love to you,' he murmured softly, watching her.

The way she had craved his lovemaking almost as though it were a drug was one of the things that sickened Jaime most about her behaviour during their brief marriage, and, in a way, his physical possession of her *had* been a drug. In his arms, she could forget all her doubts and insecurities and convince herself that he loved her as much as she loved him.

'Now, it's because I can't endure the thought of you doing so,' she responded crisply, hoping that he couldn't tell that she was lying. The proximity of him brought back memories she would much rather have suppressed. She had been shy and naive when they first met, but that had not stopped her from responding to Blake's lovemaking with an ardency that had surprised her. If he turned to her now and took her in his arms—suppressing the acutely erotic images tormenting her, she shook her head, and turned round to talk to Fern.

Blake brought the car to a halt in one of the small clearings. Half a dozen mares and foals grazed peacefuly several yards away, Fern's eyes widening with delight when she saw them. Jaime had taken the precaution of bringing a bag of stale bread with her, and Blake took it from her, demonstrating to Fern how to offer it to the ponies. When one finally deigned to take the bread from her small quivering palm, her serious little face was suffused with an expression of pure bliss.

Jaime caught Blake looking at her, something approaching pain darkening his eyes. An emotion stirred inside her, refusing to be quelled, and just for a moment, she gave in to the urge to make believe that they were a contented family unit; that she and Blake were still together.

'She's very much your child,' she said softly to Blake, acting instinctively, wanting to banish the look of pain in his eyes.

'Physically, yes, but in other ways she reminds me of your mother. She's very self-sufficient. Don't look at me like that,' he added sardonically. 'I've no intention of trying to deny paternity. Even if she didn't look like me, I'd still know she was my child. You were so physically responsive to me, there couldn't have been anyone else.'

Jaime's face burned at the implications of his remark, and trying to change the subject, she demanded curtly, 'Why have you come to Frampton, Blake? I don't believe it was simply because you want to get to know Fern. Especially as you're staying with Caroline.'

'In point of fact, I'm not staying with her. I'm renting a cottage from her. The old Lodge—I didn't even know it belonged to her until I answered the "ad" for it in *The Times*.'

'Are you saying you did come to Frampton purely because of Fern?'

Some of her anxiety must have shown in her face because he said lazily, 'I'm not going to attempt to wrest her from your maternal arms, if that's what's worrying you, but she *is* my child. . . .'

'A child you never wanted me to conceive,' Jaime reminded him hotly, glad that Fern was still engrossed in the ponies. 'She's three years old, Blake. . . .'

'Which means she and I have three years to catch up on. You say she's at playschool during the day. How about if I pick her up in the afternoon and have her with me until tea time?'

It was plain that she wasn't going to get an explanation for his change of attitude towards Fern, and Jaime sighed, knowing the impossibility of getting Blake to talk about something when he didn't want to. Part of her wanted to demand that he went away and left them alone, but did she have the right to deprive both Fern and Blake himself of their natural relationship?

'She is my child, Jaime. . . .'

'I'll have to think about it.'

His mouth curled sardonically, 'Well, when you have done, come and give me your decision. I'll wait until Friday.'

'Two days!'

'It's long enough, I seem to recall you made an even bigger one in two hours—that's how long it took you to decide to run out of our marriage, wasn't it?'

Jaime didn't know what he was talking about. Two hours! She had waited two long weeks for him to come looking for her and take her home, but he had left the country two days after their quarrel, without making the slightest attempt to get in touch with her.

'I think it's time we went back,' she said shakily. 'It's getting close to Fern's bedtime.'

'Same old Jaime,' Blake taunted mockingly. 'Always ignoring the unpleasant.'

They arrived back in the village several hours later with Fern asleep in the back of the car. Before Jaime could protest, Blake lifted the sleeping child out and carried her to the house. Her mother opened the door to them, and smiled at Blake without surprise.

'If you tell me which room she's in I'll take her up,' Blake drawled. Fern looked so right and at home in his arms that Jaime had to fight against the desire to cry. In sleep her tough independent daughter looked unfamiliarly vulnerable.

'You go up and show Blake the way,' Sarah suggested, 'I'll put the kettle on. Charles came round to see if you were back,' she added, answering Jaime's unspoken question. 'He told me you'd gone out with Blake.'

The cottage had only three bedrooms, but the third had been split to provide a small bathroom and a tiny room which could only be reached through Jaime's bedroom. She saw Blake glance mockingly at her single bed as she indicated the small room which was Fern's.

'Very nunlike,' he commented, as he carefully placed Fern on her bed. 'I imagine your dates must find it frustrating if they ever get this far, to find you're almost sharing a room with your daughter.'

'There's always their bedrooms,' Jaime pointed out, angry at his mocking assumption that she lived the life of a nun, even if it was true. She doubted that he was any monk, and it galled her that he should assume that her life was bereft of the sexual involvement he no doubt had a surfeit of.

Just for a moment, his eyes seemed to darken, his mouth compressing.

'I'll just slip Fern's dress off. You go down, I won't be long.'

'I'll wait for you.' There was an old rocking chair in her room in which she used to sit when she was feeding Fern, and he walked over to it, setting it in motion with his foot. His presence in her bedroom made Jaime feel acutely uncomfortable, and her fingers fumbled over Fern's small buttons. The little girl stirred, but didn't wake, and at last she was tucked up.

'Thank you for taking us out,' Jaime said formally, as she rejoined Blake in her own room.

'So very polite ... but you always were that, weren't you, Jaime? So polite and correct. The only place I could get to the real Jaime was in bed; it was the only place you ever lost your inhibitions.' He laughed when he saw her expression, his fingers suddenly and surprisingly curling round her wrist. 'Ah, Jaime, aren't you going to thank me in the traditional manner? Like this,' he added huskily when she frowned.

His seeking mouth found hers before she could move away, the warm, intimate pressure of it, transporting her to another world, her lips softening and responding before she could even think about rejecting him. Her eyes widened and darkened, her fingers clutching convulsively at the thin fabric of his shirt to hold herself upright. 'Ah, Jaime, this at least was always good, wasn't it?'

Blake's husky voice seemed to weave a spell around her, her mind and body acquiescing almost instantly to his unspoken commands. When his mouth left hers, she arched her throat, instinctively giving him access to the vulnerable skin his lips were seeking. Tiny frissons of reaction shivered across her flesh, a small moan suppressed in her throat as Blake's delicately thorough exploration triggered off feelings she thought had gone for ever. His teeth found the lobe of her ear and tugged on it gently, her fingers automatically curling into the thick springyness of his hair, her body unconsciously moulding itself to him.

'Jaime.' His hands slid down her body, lingering against the curves of her breasts, the pressure of his mouth gradually increasing as it moved across her skin, teasing tormenting kisses against her trembling lips, his tongue stroking their vulnerable contours until they parted in soft invitation.

She was lost, drowning in a warm, lapping sea that called out a siren song to her senses. Everything she had ever wanted or would want was here within her reach. Her fingers sought for and found the space between Blake's shirt buttons, feverishly stroking the silky dark hairs that shadowed his chest. She felt the sudden compression of his muscles as his mouth lifted from hers and dizzyingly and bewilderingly she was free.

'Your mother just called us.' Amusement danced in his eyes. 'Poor Jaime,' he taunted, 'despite all your attempts to hide it, you still respond to me physically, don't you?'

'How can I help doing?' Miraculously her voice sounded much calmer than she had expected. 'You were the one who first taught my body the meaning of physical pleasure. . . .'

'The first? Meaning there've been others since?' His eyes were almost black, glittering with a savage anger she couldn't understand.

'But Thomson isn't one of them, is he?' he tormented. 'He looks at you the way a dog eyes a particularly juicy and unobtainable bone.'

'My relationship with Charles has nothing to do with you,' Jaime choked out. 'Nothing at all.'

'No? Aren't you forgetting something?' He picked up her left hand and raised it until she was looking at the narrow gold wedding ring she still wore. 'You are still my wife, Jaime.'

'That can soon be changed,' she responded, goaded into making the declaration. Didn't he know how much he was hurting her with his careless lovemaking that stirred her body into an acutely painful response, and his equally careless assumption that she was still his for the taking, as though he had looked into her heart and seen the foolish love for him that still lived there. 'I can quite easily get an uncontested divorce. We've been separated long enough.'

'An uncontested divorce requires a separation of two years without any marital relations between the divorcing couple.'

'Meaning . . .' She was shivering all over now, wondering if Blake really meant the threat hidden in his dulcet comment.

'Meaning that just at the moment it suits me to remain a married man, and moreover that I intend to remain a married man, and that I'm fully prepared to take whatever steps are necessary to ensure that I do so.'

He saw her expression and smiled derisively.

'While you've been busy with your life, Jaime, I've been busy with mine. My first two books have been extremely successful in the States, and I'm now a comparatively wealthy man. A healthy bank balance makes a man appealing husband material. I have no intention of being trapped into a marriage it will cost a great deal to extricate myself from and, while I remain married to you, that won't happen.'

'Unless of course I decide to sue you for alimony.'

'Coming from the woman who's refused to accept a penny support from me for the last four years, that's hardly likely is it? I think we'd better go downstairs before your mother puts the wrong interpretation on our absence, don't you?'

When he left half an hour later, Blake turned to Jaime in the privacy of the cottage door and said, 'Remember, you've got two days to come to a decision about Fern. You know where to find me, Jaime, and if you don't, I'll have to come looking for you.'

CHAPTER THREE

THE next two days were hectic ones for Jaime, and she should have found that she simply didn't have time to think about Blake, instead of which he seemed to occupy her thoughts to the detriment of what she ought to have been worrying about. Sarah was busy preparing for her holiday, and Jaime herself had taken on a new assistant, a young girl from the village who had just left school and who, she thought, showed considerable promise. An interview with her accountant in Dorchester confirmed her own view that the studio was making good progress and becoming a modest success. Her accountant was in his late twenties and single, and made no secret of the fact that he found her attractive.

'It's a pleasure just to watch you walk,' he commented as they left the restaurant where he had taken her for lunch. 'I'd love to see you dance.'

Forestalling the invitation she sensed hovering, Jaime took her leave of him. On the drive back to Frampton, her mind was not on the studio and the success she had made of it, but on Blake. Time was running out. Tomorrow was Friday— the day of decision. She had talked the matter over with her mother, and as she had expected Sarah had been in favour of Blake's suggestion.

'He is Fern's father, no matter how much you personally may resent the fact,' she had pointed out calmly, adding, 'Sometimes, Jaime, I think you hate him so much now because you resent how much you once loved him.'

Once! What would her mother say if she knew that, far from hating Blake, she was still painfully in love with him? Perhaps if she did tell her, Sarah would understand why she found the thought of seeing more of him, albeit on Fern's behalf, so very distressing. It required a physical effort not to fling herself into his arms, not to beg him to take her back. As she stopped the car in front of her mother's cottage she acknowledged that she couldn't put off meeting him for ever. This afternoon, before she collected Fern from playschool, she would go and see Blake.

Her mother was out when Jaime walked into the cottage. After making herself a cup of coffee and then prowling restlessly round the small kitchen, she realised that, until she had got the interview with Blake out of the way, she would not be able to settle. Before she could change her mind, she picked up her car keys and opened the front door. It was only when she opened the car door that she realised she was still wearing the outfit she had worn to Dorchester, a soft pink silk dress her mother had bought her in Bath, its sleek lines emphasising the fluid grace of her body, her long dark hair a cloud of curls on her shoulders. She shrugged mentally as she slid into the Mini. Far from giving her the confidence to face Blake, in some subtle way the dress made her feel more vulnerable than she would have done in her normal jeans, but it was too late to go back and change now.

Blake's powerful Ferrari was parked outside the Lodge. Stopping alongside it, Jaime tried to quell the urgent thudding of her pulse. The cottage door stood open, and she approached it hesitantly, knocking briefly on the door. When there was no response, she unconsciously exhaled in soft relief. Blake obviously wasn't in. On the point of returning to her car, she caught the sound of tearing paper, followed by a muffled curse. The study door was flung open and Blake emerged, pushing irate fingers through tousled dark brown hair.

'Jaime!'

'If I've come at a bad time, I can always come back.' Why did she have to sound so nervous? Her eyes shifted apprehensively from the frown on his face, her gaze skittering wildly over the exposed column of his throat and the tanned flesh of his chest where his shirt was unbuttoned. He was wearing a pair of faded, tight jeans, and it required a conscious effort for her to drag her eyes away from the twin columns of his thighs, as she tried to blot out the memory of how it had felt to have the powerful reality of his naked body against hers. A dull surge of colour consumed her body, and she turned away quickly, hoping he wouldn't guess how desperately hungry she was for the sight and feel of him. With Blake making love had been a feast of all the senses and each one of hers now responded to his proximity.

'If I'm interrupting . . .' she hesitated half way to the door, and Blake grimaced saying, 'You're not interrupting anything apart from a monumental writer's block—something I haven't suffered from before with my other two. Come on in. It will be more comfortable to talk in here than standing out in the hall.'

Numbly she followed him into the small study. The settee and chairs had been pushed to one side to make room for a large desk and chair. An electric typewriter sat on the desk, sheaves of paper surrounding it.

'I didn't know you'd written anything other than newspaper articles.'

'You wouldn't, would you?' Blake agreed sardonically. 'I wrote my first book when I came back from El Salvador.'

Almost automatically, Jaime moved across to the typewriter. A half-finished sheet was rolled into the carriage.

'Wait there, I'll go and make us both a cup of coffee, I won't be long. . . .'

'There's no need to bother.' She said it stiffly, anxious to get their interview over and done with.

'Maybe not to you, but I haven't had a break yet today. Wait here.'

When he was gone, she studied the bookshelves behind her, recognising many of Blake's books from the flat they had shared. How long was he planning to stay in Frampton? How long did it take to write a book? She really had no idea. She picked up a novel she had read the previous summer in the paperback version, letting it drop from nerveless fingers when she saw Blake's face staring back at her from the dust cover. Blake had written this. She remembered how much the book had moved her; how she had felt for the sardonic hero; the power of the intensely passionate love scenes. As she bent to pick the book up she dislodged some of the papers from the desk. Down on her hands and knees she started to gather up the typewritten pages, her movements stilling as she started automatically to read.

The words seemed to leap off the pages to meet her, so tormentingly erotic that she could feel her body's response to them. What she was reading was a love scene that reminded her so vividly of how it had been when she and Blake made love that she felt that Blake had almost walked into her mind.

She was still kneeling beside the desk, the papers clutched in one tense hand when Blake walked back into the room carrying two mugs of coffee.

'You've written about *us*.' Her voice was accusatory and disbelieving. The previous books Blake had written, had they been self-biographical too?

'A writer uses his own experiences,' Blake told her emotionlessly, 'but you're not a naive twenty-year old any more, Jaime, you must know that this kind of sexual experience is common to the majority of the adult population, although I will admit that the adrenalin of our rows did help fuel my first few hundred pages. Perhaps that's why I'm having this mental block now—perhaps I need sexual stimulation to release me from it. . . .'

'I'm sure you don't have to go far to find any,' Jaime said coldly, thinking of Caroline. . . .

'Not far at all,' Blake agreed softly, watching her with a narrow-eyed stare that reminded her of a jungle cat stalking its prey. 'How pleasant to find we're in agreement for once.' He put down the mugs of coffee, his hands sliding beneath her arms as he bent to pull her upwards. 'Or is it just that you've suddenly realised what you've missed? Thomson doesn't strike me as much of a lover . . . I need you Jamie.' He jerked her into his arms, cutting off her automatic protest with the hard warmth of his mouth.

Her first instinctive thought that this couldn't possibly be happening was swamped by the effect Blake had on her senses. The musky familiar scent of him inflamed the hunger she could feel pulsing through her, her fingers instinctively finding their way beneath his shirt to stroke over his skin, exploring the tautness of muscle and bone.

'Jaime,' he breathed her name against her mouth, her lips parting to welcome him. When his teeth nibbled tenderly at the soft, inner flesh of her bottom lip, she moaned in pleasure, arching herself against him.

'Cool, distant Jamie,' Blake muttered hoarsely, releasing her mouth to taste the warm skin of her throat. 'When I make love to you, it's like watching you melt in my arms.'

Her fingernails raked protestingly along his back, so wrapped up in the pleasure he was giving her that she was barely aware of him releasing her zip until she felt his fingers tracing her spine and she shuddered in delicious response. Blake! Dear God, how she loved him.

'Jaime.'

She was lost in an intensely pleasurable dream from which she never wanted to wake, and the sound of Blake's voice echoed like a warning bell she didn't want to hear. She silenced it by turning her head and pressing her mouth feverishly to his, feeling the pent-up longing she had suppressed all the time they had been apart take over and dominate her actions.

When Blake lifted her and carried her over to the settee she felt only a fierce joy at being in his arms, sliding out of her dress with an abandon that normally would have shocked her. Her dancer's body curved lithely into his arms, arching hungrily toward him as his mouth left hers to trace a downward path along her jaw, lingering deliberately on the vulnerable spot behind her ear before moving downward with tantalising slowness, along the curve of her throat, pausing against the pulse that thudded at its base, lingering there until she cried out a soft protest, her pliant lips raining soft, delirious kisses over Blake's face, her hands running feverishly over his body.

'Jaime, make love to me.'

Behind the dark glitter of Blake's eyes she could see a passion that matched her own, a fierce intensity that swept aside the final barriers. His fingers trembled oddly against her skin, as he lay back pulling her down on top of him.

'Jaime.' He strung a line of tender kisses along her breasts where they met the barrier of her lacy bra, and then returned to stroke his tongue along the same line. Her nipples burgeoned into life, pushing tautly against the fragile lace, a husky moan leaving her throat as Blake's tongue pushed past the lace barrier, stroking the curve of her breast, igniting a burning coil of pleasure that seemed to reach out and engulf every part of her body. As tense feverishness possessed her, sensations which were familiar and yet strange, flooded to every nerve ending. Her fingertips stroked Blake's skin, her mouth tasting the warm salt of his throat as she inhaled the male musky scent of his body.

His hands gripped her waist and slid down to her hips, holding her against the male outline of his body, the fabric of his jeans rough against the tender skin of her thighs and stomach. Her briefs and bra were barriers she no longer wanted between them, and she stroked her tongue moistly along Blake's skin trying to convey to him without words what she wanted.

His hoarse moan of pleasure rasped against her ear. His eyes were closed; the thick fan of dark lashes making him seem unusually vulnerable, the hard line of his mouth relaxed and almost tender. Jaime traced it with her fingernail, supporting herself with her free hand, watching his lips part and his white teeth nibble on her finger, strong fingers closing round her wrist, forcing her palm against his open mouth. 'Two can play at that game,' he murmured softly, the caress of his tongue against her vulnerable skin making her shudder with a pleasure that threatened to break over her in drowning waves when he took her fingers in his mouth and sucked them gently.

His erotic stimulation of her senses demanded a response she was powerless to refuse. His skin tasted faintly salty beneath the slow exploration of her lips, her tongue slowly circling one flat male nipple until she felt the responsive shudder jerking through Blake's body, his fingers curling into her hair as he muttered a husky imprecation and pulled her away saying hoarsely, 'Let's see how you like being teased like that.'

She was still wearing her bra and the moist probing of his tongue beneath its fragile barrier was an incitement her body couldn't ignore.

It wasn't just teasing! It was torture to feel his tongue brushing so close to the aching peak of her breast and then withdrawing, and Jaime didn't think she could have borne it, if she hadn't been aware that his fingers were slowly, barely a centimetre at a time, drawing back the lacy covering until she could feel his fingertips grazing against her nipple.

'Blake. . . .' His name was a tormented protest on her lips, her eyes feverish with a desire she couldn't hide.

'Ah, ha, so you don't like it when the boot's on the other foot, do you.' He reversed their position, and now she was lying on her side almost beneath him, her fingers curling into the smooth muscles of his back. He raised his head to study her for a second and then lowered it again. A long slow shudder rippled through Jaime when, with one hand, he pulled the lacy bra free of her breast while the other dealt efficiently with the clasp at the back, freeing her tumescent nipples to his avid gaze. Strangely enough she felt none of the shame or embarrassment she had so often experienced during their marraige, when he had managed to arouse her to the point where nothing mattered save the ultimate culmination of his lovemaking, and her body arched instinctively upwards, the desire-swollen curves of her breasts rising and falling swiftly with the rapidity of her breathing.

As though unable to resist their temptation, Blake lowered his head. His hand cupped one breast whilst his tongue circled the nipple of the other, somewhat unsteadily; the aroused weight of him pressing Jaime back against the settee, her thighs parting automatically to cradle the male power of him.

She heard Blake groan and the tenor of their lovemaking which he had controlled suddenly changed, a dark tide of colour sweeping over his face as his mouth closed over the nipple his tongue had been stroking, subjecting it to a roughly urgent suckling that sent fierce spears of pleasure lacing through Jaime's body.

Almost delirious with pleasure, she was aware of Blake's hand on her thigh and her body shuddered in anticipation. At the same moment, she heard his voice in her ear, and his words were like a cold shock of reality as he muttered, 'If I'm still suffering from a mental block after this, I'll. . . .'

He broke off as Jaime tensed, repudiation in every stiff line of her body.

'What's the matter?'

She forced herself to look into his frowning face, praying that he couldn't read her thoughts; that he knew just how incredibly stupid she had been. For a moment she had actually believed that it was possible to turn back the clock; that it was possible for him to love her as she loved him. Now she felt sick with shame and shock, unable to believe the reality of her own actions.

'Fern,' she heard herself say sickly in an unfamiliar voice, 'I must go and pick her up. I don't like being late. . . .'

'I remember,' Blake said derisively. 'You always used to refuse to make love in the morning because you thought it might make you late for work. . . .'

'Not always. . . .' She pulled away from him, groping for her clothes, hoping he wouldn't guess the real reason for her scarlet face.

'I wonder what dear Charles would say if he knew what just happened?'

'Nothing happened,' Jaime said fiercely, not wanting to admit to herself that if Blake hadn't spoken when he had she would still be in his arms and their lovemaking would have been much closer to completion and, worse still, her body ached intolerably because it wasn't.

'Does he know how hungry you are for love, Jaime? So hungry that you'd even let a man you hate make love to you?'

'Does Caroline know that you make love just to get copy for your books?' she challenged back.

His mouth hardened, his eyes as dark and cold as flint. 'I never like to refuse a lady,' he mocked, watching the vivid colour run up over her skin, 'especially when that lady's already the mother of my child. We still haven't talked about Fern.'

'I . . .' She couldn't come back here and talk calmly to him, not in the room where she had so nearly forgotten all the hardwon lessons of the last few years and begged him to make love to her, as she had begged him without words so many times in the past.

'I've got to go to London for a few days,' Blake interrupted before she could speak. 'I'll come and see you when I get back. We'll talk about it then.' He bent his head briefly before she could move, brushing his lips against hers. 'I can taste my skin on your mouth,' he told her softly. 'How many men have made love to you since you left me, Jaime? One . . . two?' His eyes narrowed cruelly. 'I'd take a bet that it was none. . . .'

'I have to go.' She was out of the room before he could say any more, shocked that he could speak so tormentingly to her.

She was still shaking when she got out of her car at the playschool. Fern, fortunately, didn't seem to notice anything amiss, and Jaime was glad to discover that her mother was still out when she got back to the cottage. Settling Fern down with a drink and something to eat, she hurried into the bathroom, stripping off her clothes and standing under the harsh sting of the shower until she was sure that she had washed her body completely free of the clinging scent of Blake's; only then did she dry herself and dress again, but although she might have washed her body free of the scent of him, nothing could cleanse her mind of the mental images it insisted on relentlessly parading before her; Blake's body, sleek and supple, his skin taut and firm beneath her finger tips. The way he touched her body and her acutely abandoned response to him. But what was most agonising of all was the knowledge that he had simply made love to her because she happened to be there, and that any woman would have served his purpose equally well. Would the way she had responded to him be faithfully recorded in his book? She shuddered, glad to hear her mother's key in the door forcing her to abandon her unprofitable thoughts.

There was a meeting in the village school that night to discuss Caroline's plans to sell off the Abbey. Jaime was late setting out for it, and she rounded the bend by the Abbey gates just in time to see Blake's Ferrari emerging. Blake was driving, Caroline seated in the passenger seat, the brief play of her own headlights revealing Caroline's shoulders and the expensive evening gown she was wearing.

White-hot, searing jealousy poured moltenly through her veins. She wanted to stop the car and drag Caroline away from Blake.

What was happening to her? She was losing all sense of pride and reality. It was no concern of hers any more whom Blake chose to date. She had always known that he hadn't spent their years apart living the life of a monk, but that was before he had held her in his arms and made her body ache for the fulfilment of his lovemaking.

She drove the remainder of the way to the village in a dull daze. The meeting was well-attended and a week ago she would have been wholly absorbed in their fight against the destruction of the Abbey. Now it was all she could do to drag her mind off Blake and on to the speakers.

Charles spoke first, rather pedantically, and there was muted clapping when he had finished. Other speakers followed, and then it was her task to go round collecting names for the petition they were organising. Someone had suggested that the appropriate government department ought to be contacted and, as the meeting reached its more informal stage, heated discussions broke out as to the right things to do.

'Caroline came to see me this morning,' Charles informed Jaime as she stood at his side. 'It seems your ex-husband is encouraging her to go ahead with the sale.'

'Blake? But why should he do that?'

'Perhaps he wants to help her spend the money she'll make out of it,' Charles suggested nastily, 'after all, for an out-of-work reporter. . . .'

'He isn't out of work. He's working on a novel.' How quickly she sprang to Blake's defence. Her reaction to Charles' comment mortified her.

'It didn't take him long to get you back under

his spell, did it?' Charles wasn't pleased, she could tell by the angry glitter in his eyes. 'You're a fool, Jaime, if you're taken in by all that reconciliation talk. He doesn't want you any more now than he did four years ago. He was quite willing for you to leave him them—remember? I suppose it amuses him to play dog-in-the-manger, but he'll soon lose interest in the game once he's got you where he wants you. Why don't you divorce him? You know how I feel about you. . . .' Charles' voice thickened over the last few words, and Jaime was hard put not to let him see the shudder of rejection they aroused. She liked Charles as a friend, but as a lover. . . . Never! Her body instantly signalled its revulsion at the thought, repudiating the idea of Charles' love-making as much as it had welcomed that of Blake's.

She didn't need Charles to warn her that Blake felt nothing for her, but that didn't alter the way she felt about him.

She drove slowly home after the meeting, answering her mother's questions absently.

'Surely Charles can't be the reason for this lack of concentration,' Sarah teased mildly. 'You're miles away. . . .'

'I was thinking about the Abbey,' Jaime lied. 'Did you get everything you wanted this afternoon?'

'Most of it. Did you sort things out with Blake?'

'Umm, sort of.' She turned away quickly, hoping her mother wouldn't notice the guilty flush of colour staining her face. 'Did you know he was MacMillan Henderson?'

'No, I didn't. I seem to remember you saying how much you enjoyed his book though.'

'That was before I knew he was Blake.'

She heard her mother laugh, and realised how childishly petulant her remark had sounded. 'He used us . . . me . . .' she tried to explain, fighting to conceal her pain.

'He used his own experiences is what I think you're trying to say,' Sarah responded mildly, 'which is surely quite reasonable. Where Blake's concerned, you seem to delight in wearing blinkers, Jaime, and I can't help wishing you'd swap them occasionally for those rose-coloured glasses through which you view Charles.'

'There's no comparison between them.'

'No,' her mother agreed drily, 'I would have thought not, but you don't seem to have any problems in making one. I think I'll have an early night,' she added. 'Only a couple of days now until we leave.'

'We?' Jaime picked up on the small slip immediately.

'Henry has decided to come with me. He can't get anyone else to look after the shop, so he's decided we might as well close it down for a fortnight.'

'Henry's going with you?' Jaime was frankly astonished. Her mother had determinedly kept her suitor at bay for the best part of the last fifteen years at least, so why the sudden suggestion of capitulation.

'Why?'

'Perhaps I've seen what celibacy has done to you,' Sarah responded wryly, not pretending not to understand the question. She watched Jaime colour brilliantly and added in a softer tone, 'Or perhaps it's just that I've realised that I'm a woman in her forties, with a grown-up daughter and a grandchild, who's lucky enough to have a male acquaintance who makes no secret of the fact that he finds her desirable.'

Jaime eyed her mother narrowly, wondering for the first time whether she and Henry might already be lovers. If so, they had been extremely discreet. Summoning a smile, she said impishly, 'Well, if that's the case, I hope you make the most of it—if you don't, I might try and lure Henry away from you myself; he's a very attractive man.'

'Yes, isn't he?' It was said in such a complacent, self-satisfied way that both of them burst out laughing. As she prepared for bed, Jaime wondered why it had taken her so long to realise that her mother was a woman too, with needs and desires of her own. Was it because her own senses still aroused from Blake's brief lovemaking were more attuned to vibrations she had previously shut herself away from? Where was Blake now? Making love to Caroline? She shuddered with a chill that had nothing to do with the soft evening air wafting in through her bedroom window.

CHAPTER FOUR

'AND stretch ... and breathe ... and rest. ...' Jaime exhaled evenly, allowing her own body to relax in obedience to the instructions she had given her pupils.

If the old school had one drawback as an exercise studio, it was its lack of showering and changing facilities, she reflected ten minutes later, when the last of her advanced class had driven away. The advanced class had been her last one for the day. Today, for the first time, some of her intermediate pupils had graduated to it, and it gave her a warm glow of accomplishment to see them there.

Sally, her assistant, had left early because of a dental appointment, and so Jaime was on her own. As she always did before she left the school she went round checking windows and doors. Frampton wasn't a village where rowdy youngsters went on the rampage and destroyed property in an excess of boredom and youthful resentment, but her years in London had taught her to be careful.

She had just finished her checks when she felt a frisson of awareness race down her spine. Even before she turned round, she knew she wasn't alone, although there was nothing familiar about the heavy, thickset man standing by the open door.

For no logical reason Jaime felt fear pound through her. The man could be the son or husband of one of her pupils, but some deeply rooted atavistic instinct told her that he wasn't, and for all that he lounged carelessly against the wall by the door, she sensed that any attempt on her part to simply walk through the door would be quickly foiled.

'Who . . . who are you, and what do you want?'

How banal, she reflected weakly, listening to her own voice, husky with the beginnings of fear, as though she were an outsider, standing away from herself and recording her own reactions.

'Let's just say a friend of yours sent me shall we?' he suggested mock-affably. 'Wanted me to give you a friendly warning, like.'

The cold lump of ice which seemed to have lodged somewhere in the pit of her stomach reached out freezing tentacles that Jaime was powerless to cut free from. 'Nice place, you've got here,' the rough voice ruminated. 'Must have cost a fair bit to get it like this. It would be a pity if something should happen to it, wouldn't it?'

'Happen to it?' Jaime didn't really need to ask the question. She was already fully aware of the meaning behind his threats, but what she didn't know was why they were being made. American films and stories of extortion flashed briefly through her mind. A branch of the notorious Mafia in Frampton? It seemed highly unlikely.

'Yes . . . an accident like. People can be like that you know, interfering in other people's property, poking their noses in where they aren't wanted.'

Immediately she *knew*, and the blood in her veins almost froze, the hair at the back of her neck literally standing up on end as she felt the slow freezing crawl of fear along her body.

'Are you talking about the Abbey?' she asked bravely. 'Is that why you're here, threatening me . . .?'

'Threatening? Just a pleasant little warning like. And there isn't just this place to consider is there? You've got a little kid haven't you? Pity if anything happened to her.'

'But why me?' Jaime said it piteously, barely able to comprehend what was happening to her. Outside the sun was still shining, casting beams which picked up the dusty motes of air inside. She could even hear the normal sounds of traffic along the main road, but inside nothing was normal, and she started to shiver convulsively remembering the acid hatred in Caroline's eyes and her determination to sell the Abbey. 'The decision to oppose the sale has been made by a committee. I'm only one member of it.'

'But you could persuade that solicitor friend of yours to stop pressing things so hard. Without his support the others will soon lose interest.'

What he was saying was true, but Jaime felt obliged to make one last attempt to discover why she was the one being threatened.

'Why pick on me?' she asked huskily, 'Why . . .?'

'Why? I don't give the orders. I just follow them.'

'And what are your orders in this case?' she asked bitterly. 'To destroy this place? To terrorise me through my child? You do realise I could go to the police?'

The moment the words were said she knew they were a mistake. The man's face hardened, the step he took towards her definitely threatening.

'Maybe you can, but you won't. Not if you value your kiddie's safety. You can't watch her all the time,' he told her, reading her thoughts, 'but we can . . .'

What on earth was she going to do? Terror-crazed thoughts swirled through her mind, gathering such momentum that she was in a fever to get home and find Fern. She had left the little girl with Mrs Widdows, who had promised to babysit whilst her mother was away on holiday. 'Just remember,' the man told her as he moved towards the door, 'all you have to do is to persuade your solicitor friend to drop all the opposition and everything will be fine.'

His final words were still filling her mind when Jaime drew up outside the cottage. Fern came running out to greet her, and squealed her protest when Jaime hugged her tightly. 'Mummy, you forgot to get the bread,' she remarked when Jaime thanked Mrs Widdows for looking after her. She forced a brief smile for Fern, wondering wildly if she could possibly close up the school and go away, taking Fern with her. Blake . . . Blake would know what to do. . . . It seemed natural to think automatically of turning to him, and without thinking proerly about what she was doing, Jaime bundled a protesting Fern back into her car and headed for the Abbey.

It was only when they were nearly there that she remembered Blake could well still be in London but, to her relief, as she approached the cottage, she could see his Ferrari parked outside.

As she got out of the car, telling Fern to stay where she was, her whole body started to tremble with relief. Blake would know what to do. He would help her keep Fern safe. Blake! She had never needed him more than she did now, and it never even occurred to her that she could not rely on him entirely.

As she walked past the sitting room, she saw Blake's dark head through the open French windows. He was sitting with his back to her and, rather than ring the bell, to save time, Jaime moved quickly and instinctively towards the open windows, only to freeze in dismay as she heard Caroline's sharp, complaining voice.

Caroline was with him? Why hadn't she thought of that? He had told her that it was merely a coincidence that he was Caroline's tenant, and she had believed him, because she had wanted to believe him, but now, watching them, she wondered if she had allowed herself to be duped. Blake had claimed that he wanted to get to know his daughter, but why had he waited this long? And why had she been foolish enough to believe him when she had known exactly how she felt about Fern even before she was born? Because she loved him, that was why. Because she loved him and was foolish enough to keep on hoping that one day a miracle would occur and he would love her too.

As she stood there in a daze, she heard Blake saying comfortingly, 'Well, I shouldn't worry too much about her now Caroline, that's all been taken care of. I've spoken to her myself, and I doubt she'll give you any more trouble.'

Jaime didn't wait to hear any more. Stumbling through the shrubbery, she headed back to her car, ignoring Fern's anxious, 'Mummy . . .' as she started it up and fled down the drive in a series of kangaroo leaps which showed how little her mind was on her driving.

No . . . she couldn't . . . she wouldn't believe that Blake was involved in this plan to intimidate her. And yet she had heard him with her own ears. . . . But he had said nothing about threatening her. Perhaps that was Caroline's idea. . . . Yes, it must be, Blake would never . . . Round and round went her thoughts, seeking the avenue that offered her escape from her doubts about Blake. No, she firmly refused to believe he would ever be involved in anything like that. She knew Blake. He was so honest and upright it was almost painful.

It was only when she got back at the cottage that she realised she was no closer to finding a solution to her problem. She couldn't really leave the village. Where could she go? Neither could she give in to any threats. She would simply have to stay, she thought feverishly. She would have to stay, and she would have to close down her

school, either that or take Fern with her to
classes. Logic told her that nothing could happen
to her daughter in public and that, as long as they
remained part of a crowd, they would be safe.

If only her mother wasn't away. If only there
was someone she could turn to, but there wasn't.
There was no one.

A week dragged past, and Jaime wondered if
she was the only person to be aware of the
unnatural calm that seemed to have settled over
the village. Perhaps her fear had given her an
unusual percipience, she didn't know. She only
knew that she was constantly afraid, and the hot
sultry weather seemed to increase her fear. Two
meetings of the committee had been called. Blake
had attended one, but he had left before the end,
and Jaime shivered, wondering if she was a fool
for believing that he couldn't know of the threats
that had been made to her. If she really believed
that, why didn't she go to him for help? Why
didn't she trust her own judgment enough to tell
him what was happening? Was it because she
wanted to believe in him so much that if she
found she was wrong it would almost destroy her
completely?

Fern was getting niggly and impatient of the
fact that she wouldn't let her out of her sight. A
naturally independent child, she found Jaime's
protectiveness irksome, and this led to outbursts
of temper. Jaime felt it was the last straw the
morning she received a postcard from her mother
informing her that they had decided to extend
their holiday by another three weeks. She could

hardly write back saying, 'Come home—I'm frightened,' but that's what she wanted to do.

Every night she made sure the house was securely locked, grateful for the presence of the neighbours either side of her, and for the extension telephone upstairs. She had nightmares about waking up and finding the cord cut, and she knew the strain was making her lose weight. Despite her tan she looked ill, so much so that even Sally commented on it.

In the end, she had decided to continue with her classes, glad that the school holidays made it seem quite natural for her to have Fern with her. The little girl grew quickly bored with the day-to-day routine, and one morning when she disappeared Jaime thought the worst, almost sick with shock when she re-appeared with Sally, who had taken her down to the local park for a swing. Both of them had been surprised by her outburst Jaime knew, Sally's brown eyes faintly hurt. She was the eldest of four children, and well used to keeping an eye on the younger ones, and, although Jaime knew she was hurt by her apparent lack of trust, she couldn't confide in her.

After the second committee meeting Paul Davis arranged for them to be interviewed on one of his current affairs programmes. There was also an interview with someone from local government who pointed out the loss to the country and generations to come when properties such as the Abbey were destroyed.

Caroline and the builders were also interviewed. Caroline claimed that death duties and other large expenses made it necessary for her to sell to the highest bidder, and the builders claimed that their houses would provide homes for many more people than the Abbey had ever housed, and, moreover, that everything would be of the 'highest quality'.

'In other words,' Charles said bitterly, 'they intend to make as much money from the land as they can.'

It was three days after the second interview when the blow fell. Jaime had been expecting it, almost anticipating it, and the reality was in some strange way almost a relief, although the threat had been carried out in a different fashion than she had envisaged.

She had expected a secret, night-time attack on the school, but instead it was broken into in broad daylight by a teenage gang who had almost completely wrecked her main studio before the police managed to stop them.

They were demonstrating for jobs, they claimed, when they were interviewed. The sale of the Abbey to the developers would mean fresh jobs in an area where they were notoriously scarce; and not just temporary jobs, but houses, shops, a new school.

They had been drilled well, and Jaime knew with a sense of sick certainty that no one would guess from listening to them that their beliefs were anything other than genuine. She had been picked out as a target because she already had a thriving business; she did not suffer as they did through unemployment; she was living up in the clouds, ignoring reality.

That evening she couldn't settle at all. Several people had called round to commiserate with her, many of her pupils offering to help her to get things back to normal, but there had also been 'phone calls from some of the others cancelling their lessons, and Jaime wondered despairingly if she was witnessing the beginning of the destruction of all her hard work.

To make matters worse, Fern was being recalcitrant and irritable. Jaime could sympathise with the little girl. She was used to a certain measure of independence, and she chafed against the confinement of their new way of life.

'I hate you,' she had stormed at Jaime when she put her to bed. 'I hate you and I want to go and live with my Daddy.'

Apart from one brief glimpse of him at the committee meeting, Jaime had not seen him since his return from London. Why hadn't he sought her out? He had been quite determined about his intention of getting to know Fern better, but he had made no approach to her since then.

She had just made herself a mug of coffee and settled down in her favourite chair when she heard a car outside, swiftly followed by a sharp rap on the door. Although she knew no attacker would signal his arrival in this way, her nerves were so overwound with tension and fear that she literally cringed away from the sound, cowering back in her chair willing her visitor to go away.

Dusk was just falling, masking the identity of

her caller. Mrs Widdows would be installed in front of her television and the young couple next door had gone out to dinner, so there was no one to hear her call out. She glanced instinctively towards the telephone, and then tensed as the imperious rap on the door was repeated, accompanied by Blake's voice calling her name.

The relief was so great that Jaime felt almost light-headed with it, rushing to the door, and pulling it open, unaware of the way the light fell on her pinched features revealing the deprivations of recent weeks.

'Jaime! Are you ill?'

Ill? If one could literally be sick with fear, then that was what she was Jaime thought numbly, letting Blake follow her inside.

'Why didn't you come to the door before? Didn't you hear me knocking?'

What would he say if she told him the truth? That she hadn't answered his knock because she feared he had come to fulfil the latter part of another man's threat.

'I'm sorry. . . .' She started to shiver uncontrollably, glad of the warmth that flowed into her cold body from the fingers he clamped round her upper arms. He was frowning, his eyes dark as she remembered them from the days when she had challenged him with almost hysterical conviction of wanting some other woman, and she fought to pull herself together, her pride demanding that she didn't give way to her feelings, that she showed him that she was now fully adult and capable.

'I'm quite all right Blake,' she managed to stammer, as she pulled away, but he refused to let her go, his arms clamping round her as he pulled her against his body. 'No you damn well aren't,' he said brusquely, 'and no wonder. I'd have been here sooner if I'd known. I've been away. I only got back this evening. I had some business in London.'

'With your publisher?' she asked the question half drowsily, almost drunk on the warmth and comfort of his arms, and she wished she hadn't spoken when she sensed his faint hesitation.

'Er . . . yes . . .' he agreed. 'Caroline told me what happened when I got back.'

'Gloating over every word of it no doubt,' Jaime said bitterly, trying not to remember those words she had overheard the day she had gone to him for help.

'Where's your mother?' Blake was looking round as though he expected Sarah to materialise in front of him.

'She's still away.' Jaime explained that her mother was extending her holiday.

'You shouldn't be alone here.' Her heart leaped and then fell. Was he genuinely worried about her, as his expression and words seemed to hint, or was his concern all part of a carefully made plan to undermine her defences? Her instincts told her to believe the former, to lay her head on Blake's shoulder and pour out her fears; to have him hold her even closer, and tell her not to worry any more, but she dared not trust her instincts, in fact, she had to be wary of them because they would always find in Blake's favour influenced by her love for him.

'Mrs Widdows is next door on one side and the Hargreaves on the other,' she said as lightly as she could, disentangling herself from his arms with a reluctance that was almost a physical pain. 'So I'm not precisely alone.'

'And Fern is sleeping upstairs, no doubt,' Blake broke in roughly, 'ready to defend you the moment those young ruffians decide to take their "demonstration" a step further. I don't believe you fully realise the danger you could be in Jaime.'

If only he knew! She turned away from him so that he couldn't see the indecision she was sure was written plainly in her eyes. Once he did see it, he would soon drag the whole story out of her, and she couldn't risk finding out that he was involved in it.

'I think you ought to stand down from that committee.' His words surprised Jaime into turning round. Blake was facing the empty hearth, frowning. 'I realise you won't want to, but I'm not sure you fully realise the potential dangers here. Barrons are well known in the building industry for their ruthlessness, and they seem extremely determined to get the Abbey.'

'Even to the extent of ignoring a Government Preservation Order?' Jaime demanded huskily. On the face of it, Blake's suggestion was a reasonable one; one she had even contemplated herself, and yet. . . . 'In that case, perhaps we ought to disband the committee altogether, after all if they're as ruthless as you seem to be suggesting, we're all equally at risk, surely.'

'You may all be at risk, but not equally so,' Blake countered roughly. 'You're far more vulnerable than any of the others, Jaime, and if Barrons are behind this demonstration today, you can be sure they won't stop there. I want you to . . .'

Before he could get any further, there was another knock on the door. Charles, Jaime recognised, not knowing whether to be glad or sorry that they were being interrupted. Blake, however, seemed to know exactly how he felt. He was scowling darkly when she let Charles in.

'I thought I'd just pop round and see how you were,' Charles began fussily, breaking off when he saw Blake leaning against the fireplace, for all the world as though it were his own.

'As you can see, you were rather laggard,' Blake taunted him, his voice deep with dis-approval as he added, 'As a matter of fact, I'm rather surprised that you allowed Jaime to return home alone, in view of today's events.'

'I got held up at the television studios,' Charles explained stiffly before Jaime could protest that she wasn't a child, and that she was perfectly capable of making her own decisions.

'Oh, I see.' Blake's tone was openly derisive, and Jaime saw a dark tide of colour sweeping Charles' face. Perhaps, she thought later, that was the reason for his next outburst—one which she was sure startled him as much as it did her.

'Look, Templeton,' he began heatedly, 'I'm

perfectly capable of looking after my own fiancée, and I'd be obliged if you'd go and leave us alone. I want to talk to Jaime privately.'

'Do you now?' In direct contrast to Charles' blustering, raised voice, Blake's was very cold and soft. 'Well, I'm afraid that's not going to be possible. You seem to have forgotten that the woman you're claiming as your fiancée is still my wife, and if anyone's going to be leaving, it's not going to be me, and what's more, if you really, genuinely cared about her as much as you pretend to do, you'd never have left her alone this evening, whilst you gave a television interview.'

'Jaime understands that we have to get our campaign the maximum amount of publicity.'

'Even to the extent of arranging today's débâcle? Oh, it has been known,' Blake continued icily before Charles could protest, 'although in this instance I'll acquit you of it, but as for Jaime understanding the importance of your campaign, right at this moment, I'll bet she's wishing she wasn't involved in it, and if you really cared about her, you'd make sure she wasn't. She's too vulnerable to be caught up in the sort of terror-tactics firms like Barrons use.'

'And that's precisely the reason we have to go on fighting against them,' Jaime found her voice for the first time since Charles' arrival, and it rang with a quiet conviction that brought Charles' eyes to her face in pleased approval and Blake's in wry acceptance.

'So you won't withdraw?' he said softly, 'I suppose I should have anticipated that. You always were a cussed little thing. I think it's time you left,' he said to Charles.

'Left?' he spluttered indignantly, looking to Jaime for help. 'But I've only just arrived.'

'Claiming my wife as your fiancée,' Blake drawled. 'Rather precipitate of you in the circumstances.'

For a moment Jaime wondered if Charles would defy Blake, but he didn't. At the door, he turned to her and said woodenly, 'I'll be in touch tomorrow Jaime.'

Jaime could tell from his expression that he had expected her to object to Blake's comments, but somehow she just hadn't had the energy. Blake had made her feel protected and safe and that sensation had lingered long enough for her to want to keep him with her as long as she could.

'It won't do, you know,' he said softly, when they heard Charles' car start up. 'You'll always have to fight his battles for him, Jaime, and you're not that sort of woman. . . .'

'What sort am I then?' she demanded waspishly. 'The clinging helpless type who needs a big strong man to protect her?'

'No. . . .' He moved, and came to stand beside her, looking down into her upraised face. Jaime knew she should move away, but she couldn't. 'No, you're a woman who's learned to stand alone; an intelligent caring woman who combines all that is so essentially feminine in her sex, with a dash of independence and individuality that add the necessary spice to a sweet mixture. Sometimes, you're a woman who's afraid to admit to her femininity, who tends to hide herself away behind self-erected barriers.' He removed his leather jacket, and dropped it down on one of the chairs. When Jaime followed the movement, frowning slightly in non-comprehension, he explained easily—'I don't feel happy about you being here alone at night, Jaime, and as your Galahad seems reluctant to take proper care of you, I've decided to do it myself.'

'You mean you're staying here tonight. . . . But you can't.'

'Why not? After all, we are still married, if it's the moral aspect of my staying that worries you. Don't forget, we still have to talk about Fern.'

'Why not?' he had said, and Jaime tried muzzily to summon to mind all the reasons why it was not possible for him to stay in the cottage with her, but all the time her heart was telling her how much she longed to give in and accept his suggestion, his protection.

'I'll sleep in your mother's bed, if that's what's worrying you.' He was watching her closely, and all she could manage to say was a feeble, 'But . . . but, you've nothing to wear and . . .'

'I sleep in the raw, or can't you remember,' he derided her, 'and as for the rest, it won't be the first time we've shared a toothbrush will it?'

Jaime's face flamed. She knew what he was alluding to. The night he had asked her to marry him. The night she had insisted on going home with him. The night they had first made love and she had woken up in his arms and known that

that was where she wanted to spend the rest of her life.

'No more arguments?'

'I'll have to make up the bed. . . .'

'Well, you go and do that, I'll make us both a hot drink.'

Numbly, Jaime went upstairs, chiding herself for her weakness, for wanting to lean on him. She wasn't a child any longer; she was fully capable of taking charge of her own life, but, oh, the relief of knowing that tonight she wouldn't be alone, the sole guardian of Fern's safety! Her heart leapt and sang. Surely she had been right to believe that Blake wouldn't do anything to hurt either her or Fern? Unless of course he had been a party to the initial plan, but was now having second thoughts.. No, she decided firmly, no, she wouldn't believe that about him. She wouldn't!

Half an hour later, drinking the mug of cocoa that Blake had made for her it seemed the most natural thing in the world that he should be sitting opposite her drinking his.

For the first time since she had left him, she felt safe and cared for, an illusion she would be wise to be wary of. Hadn't she taught herself in the intervening years that it was both foolish and selfish to rely completely on another human being, and that, by doing so, one was forging bonds which sooner or later, they would find so constricting that they would want to break them and find freedom? Her type of love was too intense, too overwhelming, as Blake had already taught her once.

CHAPTER FIVE

JAIME slept restlessly, waking up in darkness to discover that it was still only three o'clock. Whether because of the traumatic events of the day or because of Blake's disturbing presence under the same roof she found it impossible to get back to sleep. Her mouth felt dry and she craved for the unique comfort of a cup of tea.

Not wanting to disturb either Blake or Fern, she went downstairs in the dark, finding her way to the kitchen without too much difficulty. It was under Blake's bedroom and so she moved about as quietly as she could. It was just as she was taking a china mug from the cupboard that she saw what she thought was a human shadow moving stealthily through the garden. The mug fell from nerveless fingers, splintering on the quarry-tiled floor with a crescendo of noise which made Jaime forget about the intruder she may or may not have seen as she worried about whether the noise of the breaking china—so loud in the kitchen—could have woken Blake.

She was just sweeping up the shards when she realised that it had. He came into the kitchen, fastening his jeans as he did so. His hair was still rumpled from sleep, the bare expanse of his chest glowing golden under the electric light. Despite the fact that he had just woken up, his eyes were sharply alert, going from Jaime's pale face to the broken mug, and then back again.

'I wanted a cup of tea,' her voice sounded guiltily apologetic. It was *her* home, Jaime reminded herself, and Blake was an uninvited guest.

'You were making as much noise as an addict looking for a too-long delayed fix,' Blake growled in response.

'I'm sorry if I disturbed you.' The kettle was boiling, and Jaime moved across to it automatically. She had her back to Blake when she heard him say shatteringly, 'I was out of bed and half way downstairs before I realised what was going on. . . . My first instinctive response was that someone must have broken in. I'm not at all happy about you and Fern being alone here—not after what happened this afternoon.'

'And you think if I left the committee it would stop happening?' She couldn't look at him, and see her fears made fact by what she might read in his eyes.

'I certainly think it would help, but I doubt that you're going to stop campaigning against the sale of the Abbey. However, Barrons are very powerful opponents.'

'And you think they're the ones responsible for what happened at the school?'

He might genuinely believe the builders had arranged the demonstration but, on the other hand, if he and Caroline had been responsible for it, he would want her to think that. If only she had the courage to ask him the truth. Coward, she mocked herself, weak, stupid coward.

'I think it's a very strong possibility, although I doubt that you'd ever get proof. They're far too clever for that. Mind out . . .!'

His warning came too late as she almost trod on a sharp piece of pottery.

'Blake!' Her protest was smothered against his throat as he bent to pick her up and then strode into the living room with her, depositing her on the settee. Just for a moment, as he leaned over her, the warm male smell of him reminding her of countless other occasions when he had held her in his arms like this, Jaime wanted to beg him not to let her go. Instead, she struggled steadfastly against the warm pressure of his arms, wondering if he was as aware of the fact that her breasts were crushed against the naked warmth of his body as she was.

A familiar heat rose up inside her, the thin cotton of her nightdress clinging provocatively to her body as he released her. 'You stay there,' he told her curtly. 'I'll make the tea and clear up. What were you doing down here anyway?'

'I woke up and couldn't get back to sleep. I thought a drink might help.'

'I know the feeling, but I normally opt for something more alcoholic.'

Jaime watched him, through the open doors, tidy the kitchen, each movement smoothly economic. During the time they had lived together when he was at home, he had always insisted on doing his share of the chores. In some strange way then she had resented it, seeing it as yet more proof of how little he needed her. They had quarrelled about it, she remembered, and he had lashed out at her saying he didn't want her as a housemaid, but as a companion. He had offered her so much, she realised now, the sort of relationship every woman hopes for, but she had been too frightened, too insecure, and too reluctant to abandon her cherished dream of conventional marriage and motherhood to take what he had been offering.

'Hey, come back. Where were you?'

'I was thinking about Charles,' Jaime lied hastily, avoiding his eyes as she took the mug he proffered. It wouldn't do her any good at all if Blake guessed that *he* was the subject of her thoughts, him and regrets for her folly in the past.

'Oh, were you?'

Surely that wasn't rage she saw in his eyes. She knew that Blake didn't like Charles, but the dark, fiercely intent gaze he was turning on her now was that of a very jealous lover.

'You're still *my* wife, Jaime. . . .'

'But that doesn't mean I can't think about other men.' What on earth had got into her? She sounded almost provocative! When she saw the way Blake's tension increased, his whole body taut with it, she knew why she had reacted the way she had. She wanted to make him jealous.

'Doesn't it? He isn't worthy of you, Jaime. Stop thinking about him. Think about this instead.' His hand slid up into her hair, twining through the silky strands, and tugging gently until her throat arched. The thumb of Blake's free hand stroked along her jaw, his eyes registering the soft quiver that betrayed her, before his fingers curled against the warmth of her throat, imprisoning her so that she was forced to witness the leisurely descent of his mouth, without being able to do a thing to avoid it.

The anticipation of his mouth on hers was almost unbearable, and even whilst she felt resentment at Blake's openly 'dog in the manger' attitude, there was a spiralling excitement and satisfaction in knowing that he wanted to kiss her.

'Jaime. . . .' His mouth touched hers lightly at first, as though he was trying to judge her reaction, and then when he met no resistance, his tongue stroked coaxingly along the tremulous outline of her lips until they were pliant and moist, already half parting in anticipation of his kiss.

It was an explosion of pleasure within her, a reaffirmation of all that she already knew she felt about him. She moaned hungrily in her throat when she felt the possessive pressure of his mouth yield, arching against him in her need to prolong his kiss.

Blake seemed to know how she felt, just as he always had. His kiss deepened to match her need, fuelling and feeding the growing hunger she could feel inside her and then, easing slightly, bringing her back down to earth by gentle degrees until she realised that she was lying in his arms, with her mouth swollen from his kiss and his lips still warmly pliant against hers.

'Jaime, you're as hungry for me as I am for you.'

'No,' she moaned the denial out loud, but knew in her heart that Blake was right. 'What on earth do you see in that Thomson as a man? He can't satisfy you in any of the ways that a woman like you needs to be satisfied. He calls you his fiancée, but he isn't your lover.'

'How do you know that?' She moved restlessly in Blake's arms, aware of treading on treacherous ground and yet unable to deny herself the pleasure of being this close to him.

'Because, if he were, you wouldn't want me to touch you like this . . .' His thumb stroked softly behind her ear and down over her throat, shaping the line of her collar bone and drawing shivering frissons of pleasure from her responsive flesh. 'Or like this.' His fingers probed the low neckline of her cotton nightdress and found the swollen mound of her breast. At the first touch of his thumb against the vulnerability of her nipple, Jaime sucked in her breath, tensing her whole body, her heart pounding so heavily it seemed to echo in the silence between them. Deftly, expertly, Blake slid the straps of her nightdress down until Jaime felt that the mere vibration of her breathing would be enough to make the fine fabric fall free of her upper body, but it was Blake's hands that smoothed the cotton free of her skin and then shaped the full femininity of her breasts, his eyes following the line of tan that revealed that all her sun bathing had been done with the benefit of her bikini top.

'Blake, please, we mustn't.' She had to take hold of her common sense and stop him now before she was completely mesmerised by the desire glittering hectically in his dark eyes. It would be so easy to give in to her own need to be with him like this, to urge him to possess her body in the same way that he possessed her heart, but what about afterwards?

'No, Jaime, you're wrong. We must.' His voice sounded hoarsely unfamiliar as though he were fighting to retain some control over his feelings. Drawn by some impulse she knew she ought to repudiate, Jaime reached up to touch his skin. His collar bone gleamed golden in the light from the lamp and she felt the powerful surge of response that rippled through his body at her touch. It was headily exhilarating to know that she still had the power to arouse him. Desire isn't love, an inner voice warned her, but she chose to ignore it. She was too hungry for this intimacy, this magic that only Blake could work, to listen to any warnings.

'Jaime, if you continue to touch me like that I'm going to make love to you whether we must or must not. Your fingers are telling my skin that you want to touch me as much as I want to touch you.' He groaned suddenly as her nipples burgeoned into pulsating life in recognition of her physical response to his words.

'You *do* want me,' he said it with almost a fierce triumph, as though there had been a time when he had doubted her desire. How could that be? She had always been dotingly, almost embarrassingly, eager for his lovemaking, so much so, that she had practically trembled with anticipation every time he came near her.

She didn't draw her eyes away, suddenly made bold by the strength of her love for him, and then as though to underline her unspoken desire she ran her fingers lightly through the matting of dark hairs that covered his chest, following them downwards until she came to the barrier of his jeans.

Burying his mouth against her throat Blake groaned. 'Jaime, you witch, you must know how I've wanted you to touch me like that. You do something to me that no other woman can.'

His admission gave her a heady power that drove out fear and shyness completely. It was as though some wild, wanton part of her had suddenly taken control, knowing without words, simply by touch, how to please and torment the male body above her. Her lips, delicate as butterfly wings, touched along Blake's collar bone. The intimate male scent of him was instantly recognisable, heightening her responsiveness. Unlike in the past, when she had been content to let him take the lead, now Jaime wanted to share the same urgency that burned inside her. Her tongue brushed the strong column of his throat and felt the tremors shiver across his skin. She teased him again, feeling his muscles clench against her sensual torment, his hands sliding down from her breasts to her hips, anchoring her beneath him, his body surging helplessly against her.

Her fingers found his belt, but it was Blake who finished the task for her, throwing aside the jeans he had pulled on to come downstairs.

The nude magnificence of his body, coloured tawny teak in the glow of the lamp, made her catch her breath in awe. Almost wonderingly she let her fingers drift over him, drinking in the sensation of warm, male skin and sinew beneath finger tips and then palms, her touch an unconscious worship of his masculinity.

'Jaime,' Blake muttered her name in a thick protest jerked past tightly compressed lips, warning her that she was pushing him to the very limits of his control, but it wasn't enough to simply feel the warmth of his body beneath her hands. Love and desire mingled inside her, raising her senses to such a pitch that she yearned to communicate her feelings to him, to pour out her love in such a generous libation that it would be a gift he couldn't refuse. Her hand rested against his thigh and she could feel the tension the muscles were communicating to her. She bent her head and let her lips drift in wordless adoration over the flat plane of his stomach, feeling the sharply indrawn breath he held until her own lungs hurt in response.

'Jaime.' Her name was a hoarse protest on his lips, lost against her hair. His fingers twined in its midnight silk as he tried to lift her away, and then, tensed instead, pressing her closer to his body as he yielded to the intimacy of her caress.

A harsh cry, somewhere between pain and pleasure, filled the room as Blake writhed convulsively against her, his body hot with the desire she could feel pulsing through her, and then, suddenly, he was lifting her away; holding her immobile slightly above him, his mouth finding her breast and piercing her with sweet pleasure.

The almost languorous need she had known to show him her love was gone, and in its place was a fierce, almost savage, hunger. They were lying side by side, Blake stroking her body with roughly urgent movements that mirrored her own desire, his mouth fiercely possessive as it moved on her breasts, his hand at last reaching the juncture of her thighs and remaining there to coax from her body the restless spirals of pleasure she had begun to believe must just have been a figment of her imagination.

'My sweet Jaime, I've wanted this so much.' Blake's voice was raw with feeling, his body shaking as he stroked and caressed her into a mindless oblivion she knew could have only one ending. 'You want it too, don't you?' Blake's tongue flicked against one highly sensitive nipple, shudders rippling convulsively through her. Lean and powerfully muscled, his body was a welcome weight on hers, her mouth parting eagerly for his fiercely possessive kiss, her body responding blindly to the male thrust of his, welcoming the heat of him inside her, moving to the rhythm he had taught it, and which it had remembered ever since.

Somehow, they had rolled on to the floor—and if anyone had told her five days ago that she would be here, making love with Blake, she would have shaken her head in astounded disbelief. But she was here: they both were, and Blake wasn't making any secret of the fact that he wanted her as much as she needed him. An explosive climax gripped her body, and she cried out his name, letting his mouth steal the sounds from her and tell her of his instinctive male triumph as his own body shuddered in paroxysms of pleasure that left her sated and bonelessly feline.

'Anyone would think we were two teenagers without a bed to go to, never mind two to choose from,' Blake muttered as he pulled her closer within the circle of his arms.

'Mine's only a single,' Jame protested sleepily, 'nowhere near large enough for you.' Her sleepy glance encompassed his lean, male frame, as relaxed and supine as a jungle leopard's.

'You've changed,' Blake murmured, his hand automatically cupping her breast in a gesture of instinctive possession. 'Before, you never would have taken the initiative. Never have touched or caressed me as you did tonight.'

'I thought it was unfeminine—that you wouldn't want me to.' She was glad that the darkness hid her flushed face from him.

'Not want you to!' Blake groaned. 'My God, if you'd only known. There were times when I used to feel like going down on my knees and begging you for just a tenth of the loving you gave me tonight, Jaime. I know this isn't really the time, but I have to say it. Leave that committee. I can understand why you feel so strongly about the Abbey, but you don't know what you're tangling with. . . .'

'And you do?' Jaime demanded angrily. Her mood of peaceful contentment had completely gone, all her earlier suspicions rushing back. Had Blake made love to her deliberately, hoping to get her to change her mind, knowing how malleable and weak his lovemaking always made her?

'More so than you,' he said brusquely, 'and what I know, I don't like.'

What did he mean? That he *had* been a party to Caroline's threats, but that he was now having second thoughts? Perhaps he had even suggested them, she thought sickly, and suggested to Caroline that she approach Barrons with them, for their help. She was sure now that the man who had come to see her had somehow come from Barrons.

'Is that why you came here tonight? To persuade me to leave the committee?'

Blake had withdrawn from her, and she felt cold without the support of his arms. His withdrawal was almost symbolic of their relationship, she thought bitterly, as was her shivering reaction to it.

'No, it damn well wasn't,' Blake said bitterly, 'but of course you'll put your own crazy interpretation on my actions—you always did. . . . You always were full of crazy accusations. I thought you'd grown up, but I can see I was wrong. Well, just remember before you get up on your high horse, that it isn't just yourself you're risking. It's my daughter as well, and as long as you're still my wife, I mean to see that someone keeps an eye on the pair of you.'

'Then I'll just have to make sure I'm not your wife for much longer, won't I?'

She could have wept. Not ten minutes ago, they had been as close as two human beings could be, but now it was all gone. A lesson to her not to be deceived into thinking that desire could in any way compare with love.

'I think I know that what's supposed to mean,' Blake gritted at her through grimly closed teeth, 'but you seem to have forgotten something—for a divorce you need either my agreement or proof that we haven't cohabitated for over five years, and you have neither.'

'Why do you insist on keeping me tied to you like this?' Jaime cried out painfully. 'What's the point . . .?'

'The point is, my dear Jaime,' Blake responded cruelly, 'that it prevents you from marrying dear Charles and anyone else from marrying me. And now,' he announced, standing up, 'I'm going back to my room to try and get some sleep for what remains of the night. If you get lonely, don't bother coming looking for me, will you?'

With that last taunting remark he was gone. As she climbed the stairs in weary resignation, Jaime reflected that she would never sleep, but towards dawn she did.

When she woke up the first thing she saw was a cold cup of coffee on the table beside her bed. In her sleep-fogged state her first thought was that her mother had brought it up, but then she remembered and she coloured hotly. Why on earth should it make her feel so vulnerable that Blake had watched her whilst she slept, when not half-a-dozen hours ago, they had been lovers?

Through her open window she caught the sound of Fern's laughter wafting up from the garden. It had been so long since Fern had laughed. On the verge of a sigh, she tensed and leapt out of bed, rushing to the window, relief warming her chilled bloodstream when she saw that Fern was playing with Blake. Whatever his feelings about her, surely he would never countenance any harm coming to his daughter, and if he knew of the threats made against her, he must know of Fern's danger.

As she stood watching father and daughter playing together, Jaime forgot that she was naked. This was what she had dreamed of for herself, a father who would play and laugh with her child, and she had tried to impose her own desires on other people she now recognised. A sudden stillness from Blake warned her that she was observed, but before she could move back from the window his eyes had roved with careless thoroughness over the exposed curves of her breasts. Quickly, she withdrew, her cheeks flushed and her temper high. He had looked at her as though he were remembering their lovemaking last night and wanted *her* to remember it too.

She got downstairs just as Charles arrived on an unheralded visit. He was plainly disconcerted to find Blake so obviously at home in the cottage, although Jaime was sure that Blake had deliberately installed himself in the kitchen to reinforce that view. He even insisted on making her some breakfast, so that Charles was forced to sit at the table with her whilst Blake moved about in the kitchen beyond.

'I wanted to talk to you privately,' Charles hissed in an angry whisper, but Blake heard him, coming through to deposit a large plate of beautiful, fluffy scrambled eggs in front of Jaime, and saying, 'Whatever you have to say to my wife that's private can be said to me as well.'

'Your wife. . . .' Charles looked angrily from Blake's face to her own, and asked Jaime, 'What is he talking about . . .? You've been separated for so long that . . .?

'That I've decided it's time the separation was ended.' To Jaime's astonishment, Blake reached across the table, lifting up her left hand, and turning it palm up to his lips. The brief movement against the sensitive skin of her palm made her stomach lurch protestingly, 'To our mutual satisfaction,' he added in a husky, intimate tone that made Jaime colour up and curl up her toes to stop the response shivering through her body.

She had to wait for Charles to leave to take Blake to task. He shrugged powerful shoulders when she demanded an explanation.

'I was simply doing what any man would to defend his property,' he said lazily, without a trace of remorse.

'I am not your property!' Jaime flung back at him.

'No, but you *are* my wife, and as I said earlier, that's what you're going to stay. Face it, Jaime, you would never have been happy with him. He would never have been enough for you.'

'And you are, I suppose?' she demanded with bitter sarcasm.

'Perhaps not, but at least I come one hell of a lot closer to it than he does. I didn't notice any holding back in my arms last night,' he reminded her cruelly. 'Your response wasn't that of a woman who already had a lover who satisfied her, Jaime. In fact, I'd go so far as to say that since you left me there haven't been any other lovers at all.'

'Go to hell!' Jaime stormed at him, hating the soft laughter that followed her as she fled to the sitting room.

'I wish Daddy hadn't gone,' Fern complained an hour later when the two of them were alone. Jaime sighed as she smoothed her daughter's unruly curls. She and Blake had argued before he left. He had wanted her to leave the committee, but how could she? Already, several people had begun to show a marked loss of interest in the campaign, borderline cases who had promised their names for the petition the committee were organising and who were now saying that perhaps Barrons' estate would be a good thing, bringing in all those jobs for the young folk, and modern, attractive houses.

She was very low on bread and eggs—Blake

had used the last of them for her breakfast—and she debated whether it would be wiser to stop in the village or go to the nearest town. She was reluctant to leave the house empty for longer than necessary, and opted, in the end, for the village.

CHAPTER SIX

'JAIME, my dear, I've heard the news about those hooligans. How horrible for you!'

Jaime paused to accept the sympathy of the Vicar's wife, trying to keep an eye on Fern at the same time.

'Janice and the children are staying with us at the moment,' she continued, referring to her married daughter. 'Perhaps Fern would like to come round for tea one afternoon?'

The Vicar's twin grandchildren were approximately the same age as Fern, and, although Jaime was reluctant to agree, Fern was already so enthusiastic about the proffered treat that she felt compelled to accept.

'You look peaky, my dear,' Mrs Simmonds continued. 'When's your mother back? I wanted to ask her advice about a pair of candlesticks we've discovered in the attic.'

By the time she had chatted with the dozen or so people who had stopped to commiserate with her over the destruction of her studio, and Jaime was ready to start back for the cottage, it was quite late. She was just on her way to the car when she was stopped by Bill Smithers, who dashed out of his office to catch her. Bill was the local insurance broker and handled both Jaime's and her mother's insurances.

'Jaime, I'm glad I caught you! I've had a call from your insurance company. They're sending out an assessor tomorrow. He wants you to meet him at the school.'

Tomorrow! Jaime thought quickly. It was just as well that she had accepted Mrs Simmonds' invitation for Fern. She could hardly have taken the little girl with her.

'That's quick.'

'Well I told them that you would be pretty anxious to get started again. There's nothing to worry about. You're very well covered—which is more than I can say for some of my clients, and Rick Brewer is a pleasant chap.'

After agreeing a time, Jaime hurried Fern back to the car. When they reached the cottages, Blake's car was parked outside, with Blake sitting in the driver's seat. He got out as they drove up and Jaime felt her heart begin its familiar drum roll of reaction. He was frowning as he opened the car door for her, although he managed a smile for Fern when she ran towards him, calling 'Daddy . . . pick me up, Daddy, pick me up!'

Jaime hadn't expected to see him so soon, and she bent her head to hide the swift rush of colour to her face when she remembered their love-making. Mrs Widdows was watching from her window as they walked up the path, and she wondered what the old lady thought of Blake's constant comings and goings.

'What did you want to see me about?' Jaime marvelled at how calm her voice sounded.

'I don't like the thought of you and Fern being

here alone—not after what happened at the school.'

'So, what do you suggest I do?' Jaime demanded flippantly, 'Hire a bodyguard—I don't think my income will run to it!'

'I was thinking more along the lines of you and Fern moving in with me—at least until your mother gets back.'

Jaime stared at him, completely astounded. 'Stay with you—you mean move into the Lodge. Won't Caroline have something to say about that?'

The moment the bitter words were out, she wished them unsaid, knowing that they betrayed her jealousy, but Blake seemed to take them seriously. He frowned again and studied her.

'What could she have to say? I have rented the Lodge for the entire summer and you are my wife, Fern my child.'

'Blake, we can't move in with you,' Jaime protested desperately, 'This is a very small village. If I do, people will think. . . .' she floundered desperately.

'That we've decided to give our marriage a second chance. What does it matter what they think?'

His casual arrogance infuriated Jaime.

'It might not matter to you,' she agreed, 'but Fern and I have to live here after you've gone.'

'And you're frightened it will spoil your chances with Thomson? I've already told you, Jaime,' Blake said in a harsh voice, 'he isn't the man for you—he isn't man enough for you.'

'I can't do it, Blake. We can't simply move in with you.'

'Not even to protect Fern?'

Jaime's heart slammed to a full stop and then started beating again as the full horror of his words sank in. She *had* been right, not to trust her instincts. Blake *did* know about these threats, and that was why he wanted them to move in with him. Perhaps he had originally gone along with Caroline's plans and was now having second thoughts. Perhaps what had happened at the school had alerted him to the reality of their danger and now he was trying to protect them— or rather, he was trying to protect Fern.

'It's impossible,' she said it shakily, too sick at heart to try and conceal her reaction, 'and besides,' she added numbly, 'there's your work; you won't be able to concentrate on your writing with us around.'

'So who's going to watch over you, Jaime? Thomson?'

'At least Charles' motives are honest ones,' Jaime snapped back, stung by the contempt in his voice when he mentioned Charles' name. She straightened up from unpacking her shopping, just in time to see the thin cruel line Blake's mouth had become. His eyes glittered, green jade shot through with gold, a sure sign that he was in danger of losing his temper. She stepped back automatically, although there had never been a single occasion when Blake had ever hurt her physically, and as though the act of her cowering away snapped the final threat that held his temper in check, Blake advanced on her, grasping her shoulders and almost violently shaking her. 'Stop casting me as the villain of the piece, Jaime,' he demanded angrily, 'and don't cower away from me like that. God, I can almost understand why some men are driven to violence by women!' He looked down into her pale face and swore suddenly, his mouth covering hers before Jaime could utter the smallest protest.

It was a bitter travesty of the kisses they had shared last night, a cold, cruel method of branding her as his possesion, more effective than any blow, lacerating her pride and bruising her soft mouth. She tried not to respond; not to let her lips soften into submission beneath the hard pressure of his; but to her shame, they accepted his touch, knowing and wanting it no matter how contemptuous it was.

'Damn you, Jaime. You make me forget that. . . .' He broke off, and released her. 'I'm going now. If you won't come and live with me, at least promise me that you'll take care?'

Her pride still smarting from the angry kiss he had forced on her Jaime snapped bitterly, 'It's a bit too late for you to start worrying about us now, isn't it?'

For a moment, a white, haunted look subtly changed Blake's features so that she might have been looking at a stranger, and then it changed, angry colour burning along his cheek bones, his eyes as bitter as his voice.

When he had gone, Jaime sank down in a chair, burying her face in her hands as she rocked back and forth, trying to exorcise the pain tearing into her. It got worse, not better. Her body craved him as it might a drug, her heart yearned for him, and her mind feverishly tried to resist the claims of the other two and think only of Fern and how Blake had put his child at risk.

There was another meeting of the protest committee that evening, and Jaime forced herself to go. The young couple next door had returned and promised to sit in with Fern. Jaime felt happier about leaving her with them than with Mrs Widdows who would be able to do nothing to protect Fern if anything should happen. As she got ready, a small traitorous voice reminded her that, with Blake, Fern would have been completely safe, but how could she agree to live with him, loving him as she did and yet suspecting his involvement with Barrons and Caroline?

Charles came to pick her up, his manner stiff and formal. Jaime knew she ought to offer some explanation about Blake's presence in the cottage, but the words simply would not come.

'We've got someone down from the Department this evening to talk to us about the problems they have to face. Do you know how many historic buildings have been deliberately destroyed this year alone?'

Jaime did not, and, since statistics were one of Charles' hobby horses, she listened with one ear to his outpourings, relieved when they finally reached the church hall where the meeting was to be held.

The first thing Jaime noticed was the drastic

reduction in attendance. There was no sign of Paul Davis, and Charles said, curtly, that he understood that the Barrons were substantial investors in the independent radio station that Paul ran.

'He's probably decided that it would be more diplomatic of him to withdraw from the campaign,' Charles told her.

So, gradually, Barrons were whittling down the opposition to their plans. It only needed her to convince Charles to withdraw and they would virtually have a clear field. Jaime shivered despite the warmth of the summer evening. Could she now expect their harrassment to increase? Both they and Caroline must be anxious to see a conclusion to the sale.

The speaker, an attractive and vigorous woman in her forties, spoke well and with great feeling about the problems their Department had to face. Their only means of punishing those who transgressed against preservation orders was the threat of prosecution, plus a large fine.

'And, of course, an unscrupulous building company always claims that the demolition or destruction is the fault of the contractors who acted contrary to instructions. Once a building has been destroyed, there is nothing we can do, and very often the profit element on whatever is built on the land is such that they can pay the fine and still show a substantial profit at the end of the day.

'I could list a dozen or more incidents where old and historically valuable buildings have been destroyed over a bank holiday weekend by a man with a bulldozer, acting on apparently "misunderstood" instructions. We believe he has understood his instructions all too well, but the problem is in tracting those instructions back to the company who stands to profit the most.

'Barrons is one of the companies we know to use these underhand methods, but we've never been able to prove it. The BBC are actually hoping to do an in-depth enquiry programme on just this sort of abuse, and if they do, we're hoping that it will highlight the problems we face.'

'Do you think Barrons will try to destroy the Abbey?' someone called up from the audience.

'I don't know. The owner is very keen to sell to them, but I understand there is another buyer—not offering quite as much, but someone who wants to keep the Abbey as a home and restore it. Obviously, as far as we and you are concerned, this would be a much more attractive proposition, but we can't entirely discount the fact that Barrons may insist that they have a prior lien on the purchase.'

The rest of the evening passed quickly. Charles drove Jaime home, in silence, speaking only when he had brought his car to a halt outside the cottage.

'In view of your apparent reconciliation with your husband, our . . . relationship will have to be terminated. I can't help wishing you had spoken to me first, Jaime,' he added in a pained voice. 'As your legal adviser, I should have been made aware of your intentions, and on a more personal note, you must have known. . . .'

'Charles, I do apologise,' Jaime interrupted, feeling obliged to mirror his formal tone, 'and, of course, I hope we shall stay friends.'

As she got out of the car she had to suppress a faintly hysterical laugh. They had both been so absurdly formal, like a couple out of a treatise on correct manners. As she walked up the path to the cottage door, she reflected that, at least, she could not now be expected to bring pressure to bear on Charles to quit the Committee. All she could hope was that whoever it was who was prepared to buy and live in the Abbey managed to persuade Caroline to sell it. That would solve all their problems.

Her neighbours greeted her warmly when she walked in, and assured her that Fern had been no trouble. Jaime thanked them for sitting for her and then, when they had gone, began her routine nightly check of the house. She had just finished when the 'phone rang. She stared at it with compulsive dread for several seconds before lifting the receiver.

'Jaime?'

Blake's voice sounded sharp.

'Blake. Is . . . is something wrong?'

'No, I just wanted to check that you got back safely. You did go to tonight's meeting, didn't you?'

'Yes.' Her voice dull and flat, Jaime gave her reply. Just for a second, she had been warmed by his concern; had wanted to pour out to him her hopes that the Abbey might have an alternative buyer, and then she had remembered his involvement with Caroline.

'That's all right then,' now his voice was as devoid of feeling as her own, 'I'll say "goodnight" then.'

The 'phone in the Lodge was in the hall and, just as she was about to replace the receiver, Jaime heard someone knock on the door, and then Caroline's voice reached her.

'Darling . . .' she heard her say, 'here I am, at last.'

She replaced the receiver, feeling acutely sick. Were Caroline and Blake already lovers? She had always known that Caroline was attracted to Blake, and Blake? . . . Blake had never refused an attractive woman's advances, surely she already knew that?

After another disturbed night, Jaime woke up late, but this morning there was no Blake to make breakfast for her. After eating a slice of toast and drinking a cup of coffee, she got Fern ready for her visit to the Vicarage, instructing her to play quietly in the sitting room while she changed for her appointment with the insurance assessor.

A tailored, soft yellow skirt she had bought the previous summer, teamed with a blouse in the same colour, decorated with pretty, self-embroidery, seemed appropriately formal without being too dressy. As she brushed her dark hair, Jaime debated whether to put it up and then decided against doing so. A touch of blue eyeshadow to emphasise the dark sapphire of her eyes, and the merest covering of soft pink lip gloss completed her make-up and then she was back downstairs, calling to Fern.

Mary Simmonds came out to the Mini when Jaime arrived, escorted by the four-year old twins, Simon and Mark. By the time Jaime was ready to leave five minutes later, having refused a cup of coffee, Fern was already expertly bossing the two little boys about, and they were her willing slaves.

'Don't worry about rushing back,' Mary Simmonds told Jaime when she explained where she was going, 'Fern can stay all day if necessary.'

An empty Ford estate car was already parked outside the school when Jaime arrived, and, as she locked her Mini, Jaime frowned faintly. She had noticed a certain sluggishness in her brakes as she drove to the school. The car had been serviced only recently, and she would have to take it back to have the brakes re-checked— another potential expense.

As she stepped into the school, a tall, fair-haired man came towards her, wiping dusty fingers on what had once been a pristine white handkerchief.

'I know,' he grinned, when he saw the look on Jaime's face, 'my mother will kill me. She keeps threatening to buy me only dark-coloured ones. I'm Rick Brewer,' he introduced himself, 'and you must be Jaime? Bill told me you were very attractive, but he didn't do you justice. You must be very upset about all this,' he added, gesturing to the room behind him. 'I doubt that any of the fittings can be salvaged. Bill tells me you've had to close your classes down for the time being.'

'I'm afraid so,' Jaime agreed.

'Well, you're fortunate in having Bill as your broker. He's very thorough, and I believe you've followed all the advice he gave you. You do have a loss of earnings policy with us, as well as general cover, which means that we will compensate you for loss of earnings during the time the building is out of commission. We shall need to see your books, of course, to estimate just exactly what your weekly takings are, and I should like to discuss with you the sort of time scale envisaged for getting this place sorted out. How do you feel about us discussing things over lunch?'

Jaime accepted his invitation unhesitatingly, and then explained that she kept her books at the cottage.

'Fine, we'll go in my car and pick up the books on the way back. I thought we'd eat at a place I know near Dorchester.'

He told her the name, and Jaime recognised it. The Belfry was a very well-known local restaurant with a first-class reputation. She had only been there once before—with Henry and her mother.

'Would you mind if I drove my own car?' she asked him, quickly explaining about the brakes and adding that the local dealer, from whom she had bought the car and who had serviced it since, was on the way to their destination.

'I can call in on the way back and leave the car there, if you wouldn't mind giving me a lift back to the cottage?'

'Not at all.'

They went inside, and Rick spent close on an hour walking round, inspecting the damage and making notes. 'There doesn't seem to be any structural damage fortunately, but we'll check that out, just in case. I wish everyone was as thorough about their insurance as you've been.' He frowned, and Jaime asked sympathetically, 'Are you worrying about somewhere in particular?'

'Yes, I shouldn't really tell you this, but the fire policy on the Abbey lapsed last month and hasn't been renewed. Of course, it is expensive to insure an old building like that, but it's taking a terrible risk not to have it insured.'

It was twelve o'clock when they left the village, Jaime following Rick's car as he drove towards Dorchester and The Belfry.

The car park was quite full when they got there. Rick explained that he had already booked a table, hoping that she would accept his invitation. 'This place is far too busy to leave getting a table to chance.'

As they walked into the restaurant Jaime was glad that she had taken the trouble to dress smartly for their meeting. All the other diners seemed to be very well-dressed, mainly older couples with a sprinkling of dark-suited businessmen. A couple of tables were occupied by farmers, looking uncomfortable in their tweed jackets and firmly buttoned shirts.

Then, as they were led to their table, a trio on the other side of the room caught her eye. She recognised Blake and Caroline immediately, but the third occupant of the table was unfamiliar to her.

'Ummm,' Rick commented, following her gaze. 'That looks like Guy Barron over there, but I don't know who he's with.'

'You sound as though you don't approve of him,' Jaime remarked, without telling him the identity of his companions. She was speaking automatically, not really caring what response he made as long as it helped her to blot out the pain of seeing Blake with Caroline and Guy Barron. So her suspicions had been correct. It gave her no satisfaction to know that she had been right not to trust her instincts, the instincts of a woman deeply in love who would defend the actions of the man she loved no matter what he might do.

'I don't. He had a policy with us—an old farmhouse he had supposedly bought for his own use. It burned down, and twelve months later he managed to persuade the local council to give his company planning permission for a small estate on the land. Not only did he get the profit from the houses, he also got the fire insurance as well. Of course, we couldn't prove a thing, but we had our suspicions. He's an extremely ruthless man, and not above straying on to the wrong side of the law if he thinks he can get away with it, or perhaps I should say that he's not above paying someone else to do the straying.'

Delightful though she was sure the lunch was, Jaime barely tasted it. All the time they were in the restaurant she was acutely conscious of Blake at the other side of the room.

Rick Brewer was a pleasant companion and she felt guilty because she wasn't able to respond to him as she ought. Her feeling of relief when they finally left was cut short by the emergence of Blake and his two companions at almost the same time. They all paused in the car park, not half a dozen yards from Jaime. Blake looked up and saw her, his eyes moving coldly from her to Rick before returning to his companions. He made no attempt to acknowledge her presence which, illogically, hurt Jaime more than anything else.

She watched as he and Guy Barron shook hands, and then ushered Caroline towards the Ferrari.

They must have made a detour into town for something, Jaime realised when she was halfway home, as she glimpsed the now-familiar outline of the Ferrari in her driving mirror, the black car gradually cutting down the distance between them.

Because of her concern for her brakes, Jaime did not want to push her small car, and she was conscious of Rick Brewer in front of her, matching his speed to hers. Blake would soon overtake them—he had plenty of opportunity; the road was straight and wide enough; and yet, for some reason, he chose not to do so. It was less than a mile to the garage, and Jaime heaved a mental sigh of relief. She wasn't at all happy about her car, not being a confident driver at the best of times. It was actually comforting to have

Blake behind her. He wasn't driving too close as so many drivers did, and she kept glancing into the mirror, comforted by the sight of the curved black bonnet behind her.

Rick had pulled out to overtake a stationary car, when it happened. Someone had parked at the side of the road, almost dangerously so, and Jaime followed his example, but, just as she was about to overtake, the rear door of the car was thrust open and a small child jumped out.

There wasn't time to think, only to act instinctively, and Jaime put her foot down hard on her brakes, appalled to discover that there was just nothing there and that she was on a direct collision course with the open door and the young child.

The other side of the road was clear, open fields beyond the hedge, and Jaime pulled hard on her wheel automatically, wincing at the sharp squeal of her tyres as she managed to pull the car round, and it careered uncontrollably across the road, heading straight for the hedge. Jaime tried to steer as best she could, hoping that her car would run out of momentum before it hit the hedge, but she had forgotten about the deep grass-covered ditch, and suddenly the front wheels dipped down and she was flung into the steering wheel. It hit her chest with an impact that knocked her breathless, her seat belt cutting painfully into her as her hands left the wheel and the car plunged to a standstill.

'Dear God, what happened?'

Jaime recognised the voice, but she couldn't put a name to it. Near at hand a child was crying, a high-pitched, keening sound. Fern ... but no, it wasn't Fern.

'Come on, Jaime, move your legs.' She recognised the voice.

'Blake.'

She didn't realise she had croaked his name until she heard the other male voice exclaiming thankfully, 'She's come round.'

'And she doesn't seem to have broken anything. I'll take her back. She'll need to see a doctor—there could be concussion.'

'I can't understand what she was doing.'

That was Caroline, her voice annoyed. Jaime could just picture her petulant expression.

'She oughtn't to be on the road if she can't control her car better than that.'

'She told me that she was worried about her brakes. She said she was going to take her car in on our way back.'

Jaime could place the other male voice now, Rick Brewer, the insurance assessor. She struggled to sit up, to explain to him that something *had* gone wrong with her car, but something stopped her.

'Lie still.'

She opened her eyes, disconcerted to discover that she was lying full-length on the grass verge, her Mini a crumpled mess in the hedge. She shuddered, re-living the sickening impact, and then winced as she felt the pain in her chest.

'Just as well you're a law-abiding citizen and

you were wearing your seat belt . . .' Blake told her curtly. 'I'm going to take you home and get a doctor out to see you.'

Out of the corner of her eye, Jaime could see Caroline pout. Rick Brewer, too, looked disconcerted, until Blake explained tersely, 'Jaime is my wife.'

'Perhaps I can offer you a lift,' Rick suggested to Caroline. 'We could call at the garage and get them to tow the car away.' He frowned, very much the insurance official. 'They'll need to check those brakes. . . .'

'Leave the car,' Blake said curtly. 'I'll make all the arrangements that are necessary.'

Jaime wanted to protest, but her head was thumping, nausea driving out the ability to speak. She didn't want Blake having anything to do with her car. Did he suspect, as she did, that it had been tampered with? Was he hoping to destroy the evidence, in order to protect Caroline and Barrons, or, even worse, had he been an actual party to it? She didn't believe for one moment they had wanted her to have a fatal accident—just a fright, and if she hadn't had to brake so hard to avoid that child, probably the worst that could have happened was a bad swerve when she tried to cross the road to drive the car into the garage, where the same garage hand who had been bribed to make the brakes unsafe in the first place would no doubt have put them right, and she would have been a step nearer to withdrawing from the committee. How had they planned to work on Charles? Perhaps, by offering him a large slice of the Barron corporate business, she wondered cynically.

'Now, just lie still, and I'll try not to hurt you.'

She knew that Blake was being as gentle as he could, but even so she wanted to protest that she didn't want to go with him, that she didn't want to be alone with him, and, strangely enough, her feelings sprang not from a fear that he might hurt her but from a dread that, in her weakened emotional state, she might betray to him how she felt, but, before she could protest, a sharp pain knifed through her, stealing away her consciousness, wrapping her in a dense black cloud of oblivion.

CHAPTER SEVEN

'WELL, everything seems to be in working order. You'll need to keep an eye on her, just in case there is any concussion. You know what to look for.'

Jaime was dimly aware of Dr Philips talking to someone who stood in the shadows of the unfamiliar room as he bent over her, searching for bruises and abrasions. 'She's lucky she got off so lightly.'

'Yes.'

Jaime recognised the terse assent, and struggled to sit up.

'Fern,' she protested huskily, suddenly remembering her small daughter, 'she's with Mrs Simmonds. I must go and get her.'

'You won't be going anywhere—at least, not until tomorrow or the day after,' Dr Philips told her, with cheerful disregard for her maternal anxiety.

'Don't worry about Fern, Jaime. I'll go and collect her,' Blake interjected.

'Where am I?' Jaime lifted her throbbing head, and gazed round the unfamiliar bedroom. She was lying in a large double bed that almost filled the floor space. An old-fashioned wardrobe stood in one corner of the room, almost opposite the curtained window, the door hanging open. She could see men's clothing hanging up inside and, on the matching dresser, was a small pile of change and some masculine toilet articles.

'This is your room.' She whispered the accusation into the shadowy corner by the door where Blake stood. 'Why have you brought me here? I want to go home.'

'Now, now, Jaime. Stop making such a fuss,' Dr Philips soothed. 'Naturally, Blake brought you here. Who do you think could look after you and Fern if you stayed at home alone? Now just lie still. I'm going to give you an injection that will help you sleep. . . .'

'My car . . .' Jaime croaked feebly, knowing that, for now, she had no option but to give in to the combined male opposition of Dr Philips and Blake.

'Stop worrying so much,' Blake intervened roughly, 'The car's been taken care of. I'm having it towed to my garage where they'll give it a thorough inspection.'

'No!' Jaime wanted to shout her protest, but Dr Philip's injection was already taking effect, and the sound emerged as a pitifully small whisper. She wanted an independent garage to check over her car—someone she could trust. A forlorn tear trickled down her cheek as she admitted to herself how much she longed to be able to trust the man standing watching her with such apparent concern.

'Wake up, Mummy, I've brought you your breakfast!'

Jaime opened her eyes reluctantly, wondering why the window had changed places, and then she remembered. Fern stood just inside the door of what, Jaime felt sure, must have been Blake's room, beaming with excitement. Her small daughter's face looked scrubbed and clean, her curly hair neatly brushed, the soft pink cord dungarees and toning T-shirt all properly fastened.

'I dressed myself this morning,' Fern declared importantly, just as though she realised what Jaime was thinking. 'Well, Daddy did help me with some things,' she admitted, obviously feeling that she ought to share the praise. 'He told me a lovely story last night—all made up— and I had to sleep in a proper bed. I liked it. Today I'm going to play with the twins again. Daddy's going to take me when you've had your breakfast, because you've got to re . . . re. . . .'

'Recuperate,' Blake drawled laconically, emerging in the open doorway carrying a tray.

'Grapefruit, scrambled eggs, toast and coffee. I trust that is to Madame's liking?'

Jaime turned her head away so that he couldn't see her tears. That had been the breakfast he had always made her as a Sunday treat—on those rare Sundays when he had been at home.

'I must get up and dressed, then I can get back to the cottage. Fern and I have put you out enough. You really shouldn't have brought me here.'

'No? Then where should I have taken you?' Blake demanded, his face grim. 'To Thomson's?'

He saw her expression, and said harshly, 'You're my wife, Jaime, remember? And you're staying here until Dr Philips says you can go.'

'No,' Jaime fumbled awkwardly with the bedclothes, flinging them back, forgetting the brevity of her cotton nightdress as she swung her feet to the floor.

When she tried to stand up, it was just as though her legs were stuffed with candy floss. They completely refused to support her. She swayed sickly, and would have fallen if Blake hadn't put the tray down on the dresser and scooped her up in his arms.

'That settles it,' he said grimly, 'You're staying here. You're as weak as a kitten. For God's sake, Jaime. What are you so terrified of? That people might gossip? So what! We are married, and you're staying for your own protection, if nothing else.'

He broke off as he caught her faint gasp. So now he was as good as admitting it. Her body throbbed with pain, and she longed for the numbing sanctuary of Dr Philips' drug.

'Protection against what?' she demanded huskily, willing him to tell her the truth, but instead he merely placed her carefully back on the bed, tugging the discarded quilt around her. She could feel the clean warmth of his breath against her skin, stirring the soft hair at her temples, setting up a reaction that was a staccato thud of her pulses by the time it reached her bloodstream.

'Would you like more pillows?' Blake had piled

the pillows up behind her, propping her up with a solicitous care that, in other circumstances, would have had her breaking down in tears and begging him to take her in his arms.

'This is Daddy's bed,' Fern told her, climbing up to sit beside her. 'Simon and Mark's Mummy and Daddy sleep in the same bed. . . .'

Jaime didn't dare look up. She knew Blake was watching her.

'Lucky Simon and Mark's Daddy,' Blake drawled succinctly.

'If you're my Daddy, why don't you sleep in this bed with Mummy?' Fern pressed, the import of Blake's mocking comment lost on her.

It wasn't lost on *her* though, Jaime thought, knowing that her flushed face betrayed her response. As Blake leaned towards her with the tray, settling it beside her, she glimpsed the green glitter of desire in his eyes and her own pulses leapt in recognition. Their lovemaking had always been tumultuously passionate, and she knew already that Blake still desired her—just as he probably desired many attractive women. Desire on its own meant nothing.

'If Mummy wants me to share her bed, she only has to ask me,' Blake replied to Fern, his mouth curling in amusement as he saw the way Jaime's lips compressed. He had no right to torment her like this, using Fern's innocence.

'Well, Mummy?' he murmured huskily, his lips almost touching her temple.

'Perhaps, if Mummy had you to share her bed, she wouldn't cry at night,' Fern continued blithely, unaware of the reaction of both adults to her artless remark. Jaime had never realised that Fern had heard her crying at night. Sometimes, she wasn't even aware of it herself until she woke up with tears on her face.

'Don't be silly, Fern,' she burst out impulsively. 'You're imagining things.' She had to look away from Fern's small, worried face. How could she pretend that Fern was wrong when she knew. . . .

'Fern, why don't you go downstairs and see what the postman's brought?' Blake suggested softly, without taking his eyes off Jaime's pale face.

'*Do* you cry at night, Jaime?' he asked quietly, when Fern had gone.

'No, of course not,' Jaime denied, hoping that the faintly high-pitched, defensive tone of her voice wouldn't betray her. 'Like I said, Fern must have imagined it. . . .'

'And yet she has struck me as a rather pragmatic child. What's the matter, aren't you hungry?'

She had been, but all at once her appetite had gone.

'Blake, about my car. . . .'

If her intention had been to distract his attention, she had succeeded, Jaime thought seconds later as he walked away from the bed and leaned against the window, his powerful frame outlined by the sunlight.

'You should never have been driving it, Jamie,' he said severely, 'the brakes were in a very dangerous state. When did you last have them serviced?'

Either he genuinely didn't know the truth, or he was one hell of an actor, Jaime thought bitterly, and the awful thing was that she didn't really want to know which, in case he *had* known, so she said nothing about the car's recent service.

'Now I want your promise that you won't go back to the cottage—at least, not until your mother returns.'

What did she have to lose that she hadn't lost already? Her heart? That was already in his keeping. Her pride? Wasn't that already in tatters? Her safety . . . weren't she and Fern safer here with Blake than on their own?

'After I drop Fern off at the Vicarage, I'm going to Dorchester.'

He didn't say why, and Jaime didn't ask.

'I should be back later this afternoon. Dr Philips said if you felt up to it today you could come downstairs, but that was all.'

Anything was better than lying in Blake's bed. Perhaps her imagination was working overtime, but she could almost believe it still held traces of his unique male scent, and she couldn't lie here all day, remembering how it had been when they were married.

'I should like to get up.'

'Bathroom is the door opposite. Would you like me to carry you there?'

Jaime froze, tensing as he pushed broad shoulders off the wall, and came towards her.

'No . . . no . . . I can manage.'

To her relief, he didn't press the point and, although she had to grit her teeth to do it, ignoring the pain in her bruised body, Jaime did eventually manage to make her way to the bathroom. The warm caress of the shower helped to ease away some of the pain. The soap she found there reminded her of Blake, and she grew angry with herself for the erotic thoughts she couldn't dismiss as she lathered her skin.

'Jaime, you okay in there?'

The door was thrust open before she could call out, and she stood transfixed, all too aware of Blake's stunned green gaze slipping over her naked body.

He recovered from the shock faster than she could, surprise replaced by a smouldering sensuality that left her in no doubt as to his response to her nudity. Her skin was still slick with water, her nipples erect, and Jaime blushed hotly, knowing that they were mirroring the arousal suggested by her inner thoughts.

Blake made a thick sound in the back of his throat, breaking the spell which had held her motionless. Jaime made a clumsy grab for a towel, shielding her body with it, her breathing rapid and shallow.

'You're perfectly safe.' The green gaze flicked over her body again, but this time without desire—without any discernible emotion, as far as Jaime could see. 'I'm not going to pounce on you. I thought you might have fainted. Dr Philips told me to watch out for signs of concussion.'

'Well, you were certainly looking hard enough,' Jaime responded heatedly, trying to cover her response to him with anger, 'Where did you expect to find them?'

Blake took a step towards her. Another moment, and she would be in his arms, crushed against the powerful wall of his chest. Her heart started to beat in heavy anticipation. Her mouth went dry, and Jaime touched her tongue nervously to her lips.

'Daddy, when are we going . . .?'

The hand Blake had extended towards her dropped heavily to his side.

'Coming now, Fern,' he called back through the open door. 'Saved again,' he said mockingly to Jaime, his eyes narrowing suddenly as he added in a lower, taunting voice, 'always supposing you really wanted to be.'

Despite her protests, Blake insisted on carrying Jaime downstairs and settling her in a chair in his study within easy reach of the 'phone which he had brought in from the hall. He had also made her a fresh breakfast and practically stood over her while she ate it. A thermos of coffee had been placed beside her, plus an assortment of books.

'Now, don't move from there,' he ordered as he left, 'not one single step.'

As she heard Fern chattering excitedly to him as they headed for the Ferrari, Jaime was overwhelmed with a feeling of loneliness; the sensation of having been deserted and excluded. Surely, she couldn't be jealous of her own child?

Blake had only been gone half an hour when

Jaime ignored his instructions. None of the books he had left her appealed, but on the study shelves she recognised the dust jacket of what she realised must be his second novel. She had read his first one without recognising that the writer was her husband. His second hadn't been published in paperback yet. She managed to struggle out of her chair and across to the shelves, despite her stiff limbs, and within half an hour she was so deeply engrossed in Blake's novel that she no longer noticed her bodily discomfort.

Set in Central America, it was a gripping story for which he had obviously drawn on his own El Salvador experiences, and Jaime felt humbled by Blake's compassionate grasp of the feelings of the peasant army described in his book. His descriptions gave her a far deeper insight into the problems of the area than any newspaper stories had ever done. His heroine, the young, initially naive American reporter, sent out by her newspaper to get a 'human interest story slanted in favour of the United States' was so well drawn that Jaime found herself jealous of the character and wondered whom Blake had based her on. Obviously not her. She didn't possess a single jot of that girl's courage or intelligence. Her love affair with the guerilla leader made Jaime's heart ache in anguished sympathy as the girl was torn between what she saw as her duty and her love for a man so much removed from her culture and background. When, in the end, they were both killed in an ambush, Jaime felt tears sting her eyes. The love scenes between them had been

pure poetry. How could it have happened that
Blake had possessed this sensitivity; this intense
well of emotion that he used so apparently
effortlessly on paper, that she had never known
was there?

When she had finished the book, Jaime dozed
for a while. Mrs Simmonds rang to sympathise
about her accident and to assure her that Fern
was welcome for as long as Jaime wanted her to
have her.

'And, of course, I can't say how pleased we are
that you and Blake . . . (the Reverend Simmonds
had married Jaime and Blake in the village
church) . . . are back together again. I know your
mother always hoped it would happen.'

Had she? It was news to Jaime, who suspected
Mrs Simmonds was guilty of a little romantic
daydreaming. When she replaced the receiver,
she felt nervously tense. Although she knew
Blake wouldn't have deliberately given the
impression that they were reconciled, it was
going to be very embarrassing explaining once he
had gone. She would just have to say that the
reconciliation hadn't worked out. Only *she* would
know just how much she wished it might have
been real.

She must have dozed off to sleep again because
the next thing Jaime knew was that she could
hear Caroline calling Blake's name. She came
bursting into the study, coming to an abrupt halt
when she saw Jaime.

'Where's Blake?' she demanded peremptorily.

Jaime noticed that her make-up wasn't as

immaculate as usual and her face seemed oddly flushed.

'Out, I'm afraid. In Dorchester. Caroline . . .' Jaime took a deep breath, coming to a sudden decision, 'I've told the police about the threats you and Barrons have been making. I know who was behind that attack on the studio—who arranged for the brakes to fail on my car.'

Caroline attempted to laugh . . . but her high colour betrayed her.

'All right, it's true,' she said defiantly, 'but you'll regret going to the police, Jaime, when they trace everything back to Blake.' She laughed victoriously when she saw Jaime's stricken expression. 'Blake's been in it right from the beginning,' she said triumphantly. 'He agreed with me that I ought to be able to sell the Abbey to whomever I wanted. It is mine, and I need the money.'

'Blake agreed. . . .'

'Agreed! It was his idea,' Caroline told her. 'Oh, I know you're still crazy about him, Jaime. That's what we counted on.'

Jaime felt dizzily sick. Never had she visualised this cruelty. She couldn't believe it of Blake, wouldn't have believed it, but Caroline's voice was telling her it was true.

'You'd better go back to the police and tell them that you made a mistake. Unless you want Blake to end up in gaol. Guy Barron's a very generous man, as both Blake and I have discovered. . . .'

Barrons had paid Blake. . . . No. She wouldn't

believe that. She tried to cry out a protest, but a thick, inky blackness was enveloping her.

'Jaime, I have to see Blake,' she heard Caroline saying urgently. 'You must tell him when he comes back that I want to see him . . . Jaime. . . .'

The world seemed to tilt forward as she tried to shake off Caroline's fingers, tipping her into an inky black sea whose waters closed suffocatingly over her.

It was the sound of the telephone ringing imperiously close to her ear that brought Jaime back to consciousness. She was slumped across Blake's desk and she reached automatically for the receiver, trying to clear her mind.

'Jaime?'

She recognised the anxiety in Mrs Simmonds' voice and knew instantly. She had heard the description, 'a cold fist clutched her heart', but had not known until then just what it meant. Something, some terrible, unbelievable fear had her heart in such a grip that its freezing touch almost burned.

'Jaime, it's Fern,' Mrs Simmonds said tearfully. 'She's gone, and we can't find her. One minute she was playing in the garden with the twins . . . the next. I've alerted the police. . . . Is Blake . . .?'

'He isn't here.' Her voice was an agonised croak. Where was Blake when she needed him? When Fern needed him? If anything, the paralysing grip on her heart became tighter. Was there some special significance in his absence? Had he known. . . . But no . . . no . . . Blake was Fern's *father*. . . .

The moment Mrs Simmonds hung up, Jaime dialled Caroline's number with tense fingers. As she had half-anticipated, there was no response. She stood up cursing the weak trembling of her limbs. Where was the telephone directory? Feverishly she searched under B, but there was no listing for Barrons. Dear God, where was Fern? . . . Where was Blake?

It was half an hour before she heard the sound of Blake's car. Half an hour in which she cursed her isolation and immobility. Where was Fern? Where had they taken her? Jaime was in no doubt that she had been kidnapped on Guy Barron's instructions. Hadn't she already been threatened by one of his men?

'Blake . . .' she was half hysterical by the time she heard Blake's footsteps outside the study, wrenching open the door, only to stand there, white and shivering, as she looked from his bleak face to the small bundle in his arms.

'No, Jaime. . . . She's all right; just tired out,' he said huskily, correctly interpreting her thoughts. 'She'd fallen out with the twins and decided to come home on her own apparently, only, of course, she got lost. The police used tracker dogs and they found her almost straight away.'

'Mummy . . .' the bundle in Blake's arms stirred drowsily. Fern's small wan face appearing from amidst the blankets. 'I went for a walk and got lost, then this big doggie came and licked my face. Mummy, can we have a doggie?'

Torn between tears and laughter, Jaime knew that in that instant she would have promised her daughter anything, but Blake intervened.

'We shall have to see about that young lady. It seems to me that people who go off on their own when they aren't supposed to don't deserve to have a dog.'

Blake's firmly assured manner was what Fern needed right now, Jaime acknowledged. She herself was poised on the brink of too many powerful emotions to deal properly with the situation. Fern had obviously not suffered at all—unlike herself, but in many ways she was a sensitive child and Jaime did not want her to pick up on her own anxiety.

'Straight to bed with you, chicken,' Blake continued firmly. 'I'll take you up and then I'll bring you some supper.'

'Mummy, will you read to me?' Fern appealed tiredly, 'a story about a doggie.'

Her bruised legs had stiffened up too much for Jaime to follow them upstairs. 'Wait there,' Blake ordered tersely. 'I'll come back down for you.'

It was five minutes before he returned. Five minutes in which Jaime managed to convince herself that she wasn't dreaming and that Fern was safe and well.

'I would have rung you from the Vicarage, but I was anxious to get back with Fern. I knew how you must have been feeling. Mrs Simmonds had no right. . . .'

'To what? To tell me that my daughter was missing?' Anger flashed in Jaime's eyes. 'Then whom should she have told? Fern's father? The father who. . . .' She couldn't go on. Sobs rose up and choked back the words, and then she was in Blake's arms, her head pressed comfortingly into his shoulder.

'It's all right . . .' he was rocking her as though she were Fern's age. 'Cry it all out. . . . My poor darling, I know how you must have been feeling. It was enough for me when I arrived early to pick Fern up and discovered what had happened.'

Blake didn't know how she had been feeling, Jaime thought numbly. He didn't know that she had believed that Fern had been kidnapped, and had not really gone missing—he didn't know that she had thought him responsible.

'Come on. I'll carry you upstairs and then bring up something for Fern to eat. Children are amazing aren't they? Do you know, the very first thing she said to me was "I'm hungry, Daddy"?'

Blake was carrying her upstairs, speaking quietly and soothingly to her, his voice stroking gently over her jagged nerves, easing her away from the precipice of hysteria on which she had hovered. By the time they reached Fern's room, she was sufficiently in control of herself to smile wanly at her daughter.

Fern was tucked up safely in bed, fast asleep, but still Jaime couldn't bring herself to leave her bedside.

'Come on, I'll carry you to your own room, and then I'll bring you something to eat.'

'Blake, I'm not hungry,' Jaime protested. 'I couldn't eat a thing.'

'You must, you're getting too thin as it is. I notice you disobeyed my instruction this morning. My book,' he said dryly, 'I found it on the study floor. Not an indication of how you felt about it, I trust.'

'No . . . I loved it, especially your heroine,' she admitted half shyly. 'Who on earth did you model her on, or is she a figment of your imagination?'

'I only know one lady who comes anywhere near to approaching Helen for courage and intelligence,' Blake responded, but he didn't tell her who he meant, and Jaime wondered agonisingly if, somewhere in Blake's life during the time they had been apart, there had been a woman he had loved as he had never loved her, but who, apparently, had not loved him equally in return.

'The book must have fallen on the floor when Caroline called,' she told him.

'Caroline came here?' His glance sharpened. 'Did she say what she wanted?'

'Yes, she wanted to see you—quite urgently. I forgot about it completely when Fern went missing.'

'Then I'd better go and see her.' His voice was clipped, and Jaime wondered bitterly what it was Caroline possessed that could make Blake rush so eagerly to her side. Whatever it was, she didn't share it, she thought moodily.

Once Blake had gone, she felt too mentally exhausted to sleep. Fern. . . . She shuddered deeply, forcing her aching limbs to carry her from her own room to Fern's. Blake had left a chair drawn up by the bed, and Jaime subsided into it, watching her daughter's sleeping face avidly.

Dear God ... if anything had happened to Fern. Gradually, the tension started to leave her body. She knew she ought to go back to bed, but the compulsion to stay where she was was too strong. Her eyes closed, her breathing evening out as sleep claimed her.

CHAPTER EIGHT

JAIME tensed, awareness returning as she felt someone touch her shoulder. It was her worst nightmare come true. They had come for Fern. She tried to get up, only to be attacked by a dizzying spate of pins and needles in her cramped legs.

'Jaime, keep still. I'm going to carry you back to bed.'

Blake! Reality returned, banishing her dark imaginings. Of course, she and Fern were with Blake at the Lodge, and she had fallen asleep beside Fern's bed.

Her thin nightgown was no protection against the chill night air, and Jaime shivered, feeling Blake's arms tighten around her in response.

'You're trembling.' His voice had an oddly hoarse undertone to it.

'I'm cold.' She was stiff as well, her bruised body screaming its painful protest as Blake put her down on the bed and her muscles refused to unlock.

'What's the matter? Did I hurt you?'

Blake knew the room well enough not to have needed to switch the light on, and now Jaime could see him in the soft moonlight flowing in through the uncurtained window. His hair was tousled, his face unusually drawn.

'I'm all right—just stiff,' she told him, and then, because she was reluctant to let him go, she added hesitantly, 'Did you see Caroline?'

His face became so shuttered that she wished she hadn't spoken. She had obviously intruded where she wasn't wanted.

'Yes.' His response was terse. 'I'll get you something for those stiff muscles; otherwise, you'll wake up later with cramp. Stay there.'

'As if there was the slightest chance of moving anywhere,' Jaime thought wearily, closing her eyes. They flew back open the moment she heard Blake's firm foot tread on the polished wooden floor.

'What is it?' she demanded suspiciously, as he approached holding a small bottle. 'Horse liniment?'

Blake laughed, the warm natural sound making Jaime realise anew how much she had missed his laughter.

'No, it's something I had last year when I pulled a muscle in my calf. It has to be massaged in. I'll do it for you.'

'He's just feeling sorry for you,' Jaime reminded herself as she felt the first, soothing movements of Blake's fingers against her skin. Her muscles seemed to relax in obedience to his comforting stroking, although Jaime did tense when he pushed aside the hem of her nightdress and gently kneaded the aching muscles of her thigh. She knew she ought to tell him to stop. There was too much potential danger in letting him continue. Already, she was acutely aware of him; already she longed to reach out and run her fingers down his spine, to feel his body clench in the familiar prelude to lovemaking she remembered so well.

'Better now?'

At the withdrawal of his hands, a surge of disappointment swept over her. What had she expected? That somehow the deft hands that had soothed away her pain would become those of a lover?

'Yes . . . yes . . . fine.' Her voice was muffled as she pushed back the covers and crawled into the cold double bed. She could hear Blake moving towards the door, and childishly closed her eyes, burying her face in the pillow so that she wouldn't see him go.

As she tried in vain to sleep, she could hear him moving about, going into the bathroom, the steady hiss of the shower tormenting her with a thousand vivid pictures of his nude body. She was so busy trying to suppress them that she didn't realise that Blake was back in her room until she glanced up and saw him standing by the other side of the bed, a towel wrapped round his hips. The moonlight outlined the powerful lines of his body.

'Move over,' he said casually.

Blake intended to sleep *here*, with her? On the verge of protesting, Jaime was silenced when Blake continued, 'It's no use arguing, Jaime. You need someone with you tonight, if only to keep the nightmares at bay. Perhaps we both do,' he added in a sombre undertone. So Blake re-

membered the night terrors that sometimes
haunted her dreams! It had only happened on
three or four occasions during their marriage.
Irrational and terrifying nightmares containing
the father she had never known—a father she was
constantly trying and failing to reach.

Lost in her thoughts, it was several seconds
before Jaime realised that Blake was calmly
removing the towel.

'You can't sleep with me like that...' she
protested thickly, wondering irrationally why she
was the one who felt the hot flush of embarrassment, and dragged her eyes away. Out of the
corner of her eye, she saw Blake's brief shrug.

'Don't be silly, Jaime. I always sleep this way,
you should know that.'

She felt the bed depress as he got in beside her
and held her body taut, creeping as close to her
edge as she could without falling off; her breath
held in her chest in a painfully tight ball.

Almost within minutes, Blake was asleep, the
even rise and fall of his breathing calming the
heavy thud of her heart. Beneath the covers she
could feel the heat of his body reaching out to
her, warming her chilled back. More than
anything else on earth, she wanted to turn round
and creep closer to him, cuddling up to him as
she used to do. The harder she fought the
compulsion, the stronger it grew, until, at last,
with a small groan of self-contempt, she turned
over, drawn inexorably towards Blake's warm
back.

Some time later, Jaime was drowsily aware of

Blake turning over, in his sleep, his arm automatically curving below her breasts and round her back as he settled more comfortably against the contours of her body. Jaime knew she ought to move away, but the temptation to stay where she was was too great. Ignoring all the urgings of common sense which told her she ought to move while she still could, she nestled closer to Blake's warm body. The hand that had been supporting the small of her back moved to cup her breast. Jaime tensed as Blake moved in his sleep, her mind a complete blank as she tried to find an excuse to explain away her presence in his arms if he should wake. Panic stealing away her previous contentment, she tried to move, and found that she could not. Blake growled protestingly in his sleep, his hand closing more possessively on her body.

'Jaime?'

Jaime tensed as she heard the sleep-slurred question in his voice. 'Why on earth are you wearing this damned thing?' Blake continued. 'You know I like to feel you against me.'

He thought they were still living together, was Jaime's first agonised thought. Still drugged by sleep, Blake believed they were still lovers.

'Blake . . .' she protested uncertainly, 'Blake. . . .'

'Umm. I'm here.' He nuzzled the vulnerable arch of her throat, his free hand curling around it, his fingers stroking gently across her skin.

Tiny fires started to burn wherever he touched, and Jaime shivered in mute response, knowing she should wake him up properly and stop him, and yet, despairingly, knowing at the same time that she was too weak to do so. She was here, in his arms, where she had longed to be so often in the long years they had been apart, her body already craving more than the gentle drift of his fingers against her skin and the warmth of his mouth tracing lazy kisses along her jaw.

The fingers that had been tugging at her nightgown finally worked it free of her arm, and then returned to cup the smooth pale flesh of the breast they had exposed.

His touch was as light as a sigh, Jaime thought lost in a daze of pleasure, and as potentially dangerous as dynamite. She stretched out her hand, genuinely intending to push him away, but the moment her fingers came into contact with the smooth wall of his chest, the touch she had intended as a repudiation became a hesitant caress.

Beneath her fingertips she could feel his soft body hair, and, as though magnetised to it, her fingers stole downwards.

'Umm, that's good.'

Jaime tensed. Her senses responding against her will to the husky, male appreciation in Blake's voice. Confined by the warmth of his hand, she could feel her breast swelling yearningly, shuddering when Blake stroked his thumb softly against her nipple in recognition of her arousal.

'Touch me again, Jaime.' His voice seemed to come from deep inside him, a sensual purr that she could feel reverberating through his body. 'Let's get this thing off.'

Deft hands tugged the whole nightie off. Blake wasn't anywhere near halfway asleep now, and must know that they were no longer living as man and wife, but it was as though a spell had been put on Jaime's speech, preventing her from bringing it to his attention. Instead she gazed bemusedly up at him as he lowered her back against the mattress, gently holding her hands at her sides as she automatically tried to conceal her nakedness from him.

'No, let me look.'

His gaze was almost a caress in itself, leaving her pliant and trembling, feeling that her body was a precious sacrifice that she must yield up to him.

'Jaime.' Her name left his lips on a whisper, as he kneeled beside her, bending over her until his body blocked out the light, cupping her face gently in both hands as he kissed her.

The touch of his lips was almost tentative, searching, delicate, almost as though she were some timid woodland creature he was frightened of chasing away. Indeed, in many ways, his hesitant caress was more seductive than a more fiercely passionate demand because it gave Jaime the confidence to relax, to let her lips and body flower into ripe awareness, like a flower opening up to the sun.

Gradually, the pressure of Blake's kiss increased, but Jaime was barely aware of it doing so. All of her was concentrated on responding in counter to the fiercely sweet music Blake was playing. In concert, they seemed to move together, her mouth opening, her tongue tasting, her body yielding even before Blake touched it.

Gently releasing her mouth, Blake commanded huskily,

'Open your eyes.'

Obediently, Jaime did so, meeting the green depths of Blake's. It was almost as though he hypnotised her; as though she were unable to withdraw her gaze from his as he released her face and slowly stroked his fingers down her throat. Jaime raised her hands, automatically wanting to touch him, but Blake shook his head and said softly, 'Not yet.'

He had reached the valley between her breasts, cupping them both. Trembling with tension, Jaime followed his gaze down her body. His eyes seemed to smoulder as he studied the twin pink crests. When he bent his head and slowly anointed each burgeoning nipple with the moist warmth of his mouth, Jaime shuddered in helpless reaction, her self-control splintering.

'Blake.' He made no move to stop her when her arms tightened round him, her trembling mouth pressing wild kisses against his skin. Where it had simply felt comfortingly warm when she had cuddled against him, now it burned. His mouth scorched her skin as tenderness gave way to passion, forcing her to cry out his name and be granted the immediate surcease of the caresses her body craved. Everything about him was familiar, and yet achingly exciting. His hand stroking her thigh made her arch and ache with pleasure, his mouth against her breast unleashing the husky cries of need he seemed so hungry to hear.

In a frenzy of arousal, Jaime mimicked his caresses. Her tongue found and brushed his flat, male nipples, her hand stroked the smooth skin of his belly, the kisses she placed there making him groan and reach for her.

'Dear God, Jaime,' Blake muttered rawly into her parted mouth, 'If this is what it results in, I'll have to arrange for Fern to go missing more often.'

If the earth had rocked beneath her, it couldn't have had a more cataclysmic effect on Jaime. Her body tensed, her voice hoarse with pain, she said thickly, 'Don't you mean "again"? I know all about it Blake,' she continued bleakly, 'all about how you agreed with Caroline; how the three of you worked out your plan. You wanted Charles to leave the committee, and you thought you could get him to do it through me, hence that attack on the school, my wonky brakes ... but to threaten to hurt Fern ... your own child. I know you never wanted her, but. ...' She was crying, forcing the bleak words out between sobs, wondering how she had ever found Blake's body warm and secure. Now she could almost feel the icy cold coming off it, freezing through her.

'Say that again. ...' His voice sounded completely flat, almost dangerous in some strange way.

'I know you never wanted Fern,' Jaime hiccoughed.

'No, not that. . . . All that rubbish about Caroline and me.'

'It isn't rubbish. I didn't want to believe it . . . but Caroline told me the truth this afternoon, when I threatened her with the police.'

'And when Fern went missing, you thought. . . .' Blake began slowly.

'I thought that your threat had been carried out. That's what the man who came to the school told me . . . but I couldn't believe. . . .'

'But you *did* believe, didn't you?' Blake said furiously angry. 'You believed I was a party to this harrassment of you . . . that I would actually condone behaviour which could hurt my own child. No wonder you left me, Jaime,' he said bitterly, 'I never realised before quite how low your opinion of me was. Well, for your information, until now I had no idea you were being threatened.'

'You mean, you didn't know about why the school was attacked and my brakes tampered with?' Hope flared inside her, only to die as she saw Blake's momentary hesitation.

'I certainly had no part in it,' he said at last, but Jaime had not received the answer she had wanted. Blake *had* known, and knowing had done nothing to stop it.

'Blake, I think it's best if Fern and I go home tomorrow,' she said tiredly.

'No!' The sharp denial pierced through her. 'No, Jaime, you're both staying where you are, or are you frightened that I might do the pair of you further harm, poison perhaps. . . .'

'No . . . no . . . of course not. . . .'

'Right then, you're both staying here, at least until your mother gets back. You can hardly think I'd let any harm come to you under my own roof,' he added sardonically. 'Work it out for yourself, Jaime. If I am as involved with Caroline's machinations as you seem to think, then you're safer here than anywhere else.'

'And *are* you involved?' She held her breath, waiting for the answer. Only she knew how much she longed for him to deny it, but, to her anguish, he slid out of bed, leaning towards her.

'Have you so little faith in me that you need to ask, Jaime? Some wife you are . . . but then, you never did trust me, did you?'

'Because you never gave me reason to. . . .' Jaime cried out in pain.

'Trust shouldn't need reasons,' Blake responded bitterly. 'Like love, it should be given freely. I'll go back to my own room now. You needn't worry that I'll bother you again, Jaime.'

He spoke with such an air of finality that Jaime was confused. It was almost as though, in his eyes, he was the injured party, but how could that be?

The next day, Jaime barely saw him. She heard him outside with Fern, the little girl laughing as they played, but, apart from asking her if she was feeling well enough to be downstairs, he said nothing to her. Once she had assured him that she was, he abandoned Fern into her care and shut himself in his study. The closed door seemed in some way symbolic, and Jaime felt as though he had deliberately closed it against her, shutting her out of his life. In some strange way, she felt as guilty as though she had let him down, but, surely, he was the guilty one? Hadn't she given him every opportunity to deny his involvement with Caroline and Barrons? Trust should be given freely, as he had said, and Jaime had known he wasn't talking purely about the present, but, in the past, she hadn't had the self-confidence to trust in her own ability to keep his love. And neither had she trusted him to go on loving her. *Had* she been wrong? But no . . . Suzy had made it plain that he had grown bored with her. He hadn't even loved her enough to give up his job and settle down, and yet no sooner had he come back from El Salvador than he had given up newspaper reporting. Too muddled to think any further, Jaime went out into the garden to play with Fern.

'I like living with my Daddy,' the little girl told her. 'Do you, Mummy?'

What could she say?

'I want to live with him for always,' Fern protested. 'Can we, Mummy?'

How on earth was she supposed to answer her daughter? How could she explain to her that Blake probably didn't want either of them?

Mrs Simmonds called round late in the afternoon, breathless and apologetic.

'You must have been frantic when I rang you about Fern. I was myself. They say these things come in threes don't they?' she continued. 'First your accident, and then Fern getting lost.'

Jaime shivered. 'Let's hope that this time they're wrong,' she said lightly, but she felt apprehensive nevertheless, and oddly glad that she had given in to Blake and stayed at the Lodge.

When six o'clock came and went, and Blake was still working, Jaime gave Fern her tea. She had found a chicken in the freezer and casseroled it, and now a tempting aroma filled the small kitchen. There had been enough gooseberries on the half-wild bushes to make a pie, and Fern's appetite did not seem to have diminished by her adventure because she ate well, which was more than she could do, Jaime reflected watching her.

Blake's portion she put on a tray, which she placed outside the study door, simply calling out, 'Food's outside for you, Blake,' and then walking away.

She was just putting Fern to bed when she heard a dull ominous rumbling. The sound seemed to fill the room, it almost seemed as though the Lodge was shaking to its foundations, rather like an underground thunderstorm, Jaime thought hazily rushing to the window. What could it be? Surely, not an earthquake? Chiding herself for being silly, she searched the sky for signs of thunder, but there weren't any. It was clear, soft blue, the sun just beginning to set. A band of parkland hid the bulk of the Abbey from her view and, although the sound seemed to be coming from that direction, Jaime could see nothing at all.

She was halfway downstairs when she heard the 'phone ring. The tray had disappeared from outside the study, but Blake was obviously still inside because he answered the 'phone almost straight away.

Seconds later, Jaime almost collided with him as he hurried out, pulling on his leather jerkin as he did so.

'I've got to get up to the Abbey,' he told her tersely. 'Stay here and keep the door locked until I get back.'

Before she could question him further, he was gone. Jaime was surprised to see him running through the garden, using the old track that ran from the Lodge to the house. If he was in such a rush, why wasn't he using the Ferrari? Obedient to his instructions, she locked and barred the old-fashioned door, checking that the French windows in the study were closed and locked. Fear shivered through her. What was happening? Why had he gone to the Abbey?

She had almost given up all hope of him returning when he eventually came back. She was sitting in the kitchen, and his brief rap on the door startled her.

'Jaime, open up, it's me, Blake,' he commanded tersely. When Jaime opened the door, she was surprised to see smudges of dirt on his face. His jacket had been torn, and there were more smears of dirt on his shirt.

'Make me a cup of coffee, would you?' he asked tiredly, dropping into a chair.

Jaime was longing to ask him why he had gone

to the Abbey, but pride put a guard on her
tongue. As she handed him a mug of coffee she
noticed that the skin across the knuckles of his
right hand was split and bleeding. Her small gasp
of alarm drew Blake's attention to his hand.

'What happened?'

'Nothing,' he told her brusquely, 'Look, I'm
tired. I think I'll go to bed if you don't mind. I
need an early start in the morning. I have to go to
London.'

Never before had he rejected her so coldly.
Jaime was still recoiling from the shock of it
when he left the kitchen. Well, what had she
expected, she wondered bitterly, automatically
rinsing their empty mugs. That he would be so
thrilled to find she had waited up for him so that
he would take her in his arms and . . . 'Oh, stop it,'
she urged herself. 'Stop hurting yourself. You
know he doesn't love you.'

She was awake in time to see him leaving in the
morning. It was the sound of the Ferrari that
woke her, but, as she hurried to the window, it
was towards the Abbey that he was driving—not
away from it. Ten minutes later, the powerful
black car reappeared, but this time Blake wasn't
the only passenger. Caroline was sitting beside
him.

A despair such as she had never known before
overwhelmed Jaime. She couldn't stay in the
Lodge a moment longer she decided. She would
have to go home.

She was just on the verge of telephoning for a
taxi when the sound of a car took her to the

window. An unfamiliar saloon car was pulling up outside the Lodge. Someone was getting out. Her mother, Jaime recognised on a wave of disbelief, and Henry; and what was more, they were holding hands and looking at one another for all the world as though. . . . In a daze, she opened the door.

'Darling,' her mother carolled, 'Guess what?' She brandished her left hand, displaying the brand new engagement and wedding rings.

'But. . . .'

'Let's go inside and have a cup of tea,' Henry suggested practically, 'and we'll tell you all about it. I must say, if I'd known the softening effect it was likely to have on her, I'd have taken your mother to Rome years ago.'

'You're married!' Jaime exclaimed stupidly, as she filled the kettle, 'but. . . .'

'By special licence, my dear, no less,' Sarah announced, grinning.

'Yes, once she agreed to marry me, I couldn't risk her changing her mind,' Henry put in. 'I got everything arranged as quickly as I could and we flew into London yesterday. Just in time to tie the knot.'

'We would have loved you to have been there, darling,' her mother broke in, 'but when I 'phoned Blake, he explained how bruised and battered you were.'

'You 'phoned Blake,' Jaime gasped, 'but. . . .'

'Well, at first, I rang the cottage, and then, when I couldn't get any reply, I 'phoned Mrs Widdows. She told me you and Blake were back together, so naturally, I rang him. I asked him to keep our news a surprise though, so that we could tell you ourselves. Not that I'm the only one keeping secrets, and I can't tell you how happy I am about yours, darling. You were never somehow complete without Blake, and I always wondered if you hated him quite as much as you professed to.'

'Mother. . . .' Jaime tried to break into her mother's excited conversation to tell her the truth, but Henry forestalled her, dropping a bombshell which stunned her. 'Actually, we're rather glad about the reconciliation for selfish reasons. Your mother and I have decided to move to Bath. I have a friend there who's selling his antique business. It's a very good one, but rather pricey, but with what we'll get for ours, plus the sale of the cottage, we should have enough.'

Jaime just didn't know what to say. With one blow, she was losing everything, and Mrs Simmonds' pessimistic pronouncement came back to her. While she tried to recover from the blow, she was aware of her mother and Henry glowing like a pair of teenagers, no doubt waiting for her congratulations.

Pulling herself together, Jaime hugged and kissed them both, chiding herself for her selfishness. Of course, she was pleased to see them, it was just that she hadn't bargained for losing her mother and her home quite so unexpectedly. Another thought struck her. How could she tell them the truth about Blake and herself now? If she did, her mother would immediately realise that she had no home to go to. No, Jaime thought determinedly, she mustn't spoil their happiness. It would mean asking Blake to participate in the charade but, hopefully, not for very long. She would have to find lodgings for herself and Fern somewhere in the village eventually, which wouldn't be easy, and she would have to work even harder at the studio. Not for the first time, Jaime recognised how much she had relied on her mother's support, both moral and financial. What if Blake wouldn't agree? Jaime could hardly bear to think about it. He *had* to. He *had* to. All at once, she was in a fever of impatience for him to get back.

'Where is Blake, by the way?' her mother asked.

'In London—on business. . . .'

'Well, we won't stay. We just wanted to give you our good news. Henry wants to take us all out to dinner on Sunday—a post-wedding celebration. We're staying at the cottage tonight. . . .'

'I'll come round tomorrow then, and we'll have a chat,' Jaime responded. 'Most of our things are still there. . . .'

'Yes, Blake told me the Lodge was only a temporary arrangement,' her mother agreed, bending to kiss both Jaime and Fern who had been listening to the adult conversation with great interest.

'Are you now my grandpa?' she astounded them all by asking Henry as they prepared to leave.

'Do you want me to be?'

'Yes,' she said, with such simple enthusiasm that they all laughed. Henry picked her up until their faces were level, 'Then I will be.'

'Now I've got a daddy and a grandpa,' she exclaimed, with very evident relish, when Henry put her down.

The Lodge seemed unappealingly quiet when they had gone. Just what had she got herself into, Jaime wondered, in a fever of torment for Blake to return. If he refused to help her, what on earth was she going to do? How did he really feel about Caroline? He had not mentioned divorce, and yet he seemed eager to rush to Caroline's side at her slightest bidding. He had wanted her to stay at the Lodge, and yet he had not denied that he had been involved in those threats against her. Sighing, Jaime walked round the Lodge.

She had put Fern to bed, and now time seemed to drag as she waited for Blake to return. She wandered into his study and curled up in his deep leather chair, finding comfort in the faint scent of his body which clung to the leather.

CHAPTER NINE

'JAIME?'

Jaime opened her eyes muzzily. She could hear feet pounding down the stairs.

'In here, Blake,' she called out, stretching stiff limbs and glancing at her watch. Eleven o'clock! Could she really have been asleep that long? The handle of the study door turned, and Blake walked in. His eyebrows met in a heavy frown, a look she was unfamiliar with shadowing his eyes.

'I thought you'd left.'

'Without Fern? I was waiting up for you. . . .'

'How flattering.' He seemed to be in a strange mood, moving restlessly round the room, picking up and then discarding various articles.

'Jaime.'

'Blake.'

They both spoke together.

'Ladies first.' Blake made her a brief bow.

Now that the moment was here, Jaime just didn't know what to say. 'Blake, please let me live here so that my mother thinks we've been reconciled.'? 'Blake, my mother thinks. . . .'?

'Blake.' Her voice cracked over his, and she tried again. 'Blake, my mother came round this afternoon.'

He had been reaching for the decanter that stood on the shelf and now his hand stilled. 'Yes?'

The word was curiously without any depth of emotion, as though he was deliberately trying to give off a calm he was far from feeling.

Jaime took a deep breath.

'I know you know about her marriage. I'm pleased for them both, of course, but there are problems.' She risked a look into his face, and wished she hadn't when she saw the brooding darkness there.

'She ... that is, they ... believe that we're reconciled, and she wants to sell the cottage.' It all came out in a rush with Jaime nervously twisting her fingers together. 'Blake, I. . . .'

'And?'

Dear God, how on earth was she going to ask him? In the end, there was only one way. 'And I was hoping you would agree to let Fern and me live here with you—as though we *were* reconciled,' she added baldly, so that there couldn't be any misunderstanding, 'at least, until they sell the cottage. They need the money, you see,' she added desperately, 'they want to buy a business and move to Bath, but if mother thinks she has to be responsible for Fern and me. . . .'

'As opposed to thinking *I* am responsible for you, I suppose you mean. . . . Do you honestly realise what you're asking me, Jaime?'

'Yes.' How small and weak her voice sounded as she shrank beneath the biting lash of his voice.

'Yesterday, you couldn't wait to get away from me, and yet now you're telling me that you want to stay.'

'I realise it's an imposition, Blake.' Suddenly

her courage returned, 'But if you hadn't dragged me here in the first place, no one would have thought we were reconciled. . . .'

'And that being the case, it is incumbent upon me to see that the deception continues. Very well. . . .'

'You mean . . . you mean we can stay?'

'Yes.'

He had his back to her, and Jaime couldn't see his face, but his voice was as cold as arctic ice.

'And now, if you don't mind, I'd like my study to myself for a while. I've got some clearing up to do.'

Knowing that she was being dismissed Jaime walked out of the room on very unsteady legs. Blake had agreed to her request, but, instead of feeling relieved, all she could feel was an aching emptiness.

'Look, Mummy, a picture of Daddy,' Fern flung herself on to the bed, thrusting the local paper under Jaime's nose. She picked it up, reading the headline in disbelief.

'Well-known writer and local police foil attempt to destroy building of historical importance.' As her eyes slid over the printed lines, Jaime felt as though she had strayed into a completely unfamiliar world, one in which Caroline had apparently been intimidated by Barrons into agreeing to sell them the Abbey, only to change her mind and decide instead to sell it to another buyer—someone who wasn't named but who wished to keep the Abbey as a private home and preserve it. Blake had apparently played along with Barrons, pretending to support their plans in order to gain inside information on them.

The news that a bulldozer had been driven into the Abbey grounds had alerted the police to the fact that Barrons had decided to take matters into their own hands and force Caroline to sell to them by destroying part of the building. Blake, summoned by a terrified Caroline, had succeeded in knocking out the bulldozer driver, and preventing any damage, before the police arrived to take control.

Jaime put down the paper with a white face, scraps of conversation returning to mock her. 'Are you involved . . .?' she had said, and Blake had avoided answering her. 'Trust should be given freely,' he had said, and she had not understood, had not wanted to understand. Blake had known because of his self-appointed role, and, knowing, had tried his best to protect Fern and herself by taking them into his own home. That was why he had insisted on them moving to the Lodge, not because he particularly wanted them there.

As Jaime heard his footsteps on the stairs, shame washed over her, and then pride came to her rescue.

'I see you're quite a hero,' she announced gaily, as he walked in, carrying a mug of coffee.

'The local rag's made it all seem much more important than it was. I knew about Barrons' reputation from a documentary a friend of mine in television had been working on. As soon as I put Caroline wise, she began to have second thoughts about selling to them, especially as there was another . . . interested party, but she couldn't withdraw very easily. You weren't the only one to be threatened by Barrons' strong-arm team.'

'And the bulldozer?'

'A rather hackneyed method of getting rid of unwanted old buildings. Barrons no doubt thought that knocking down a wall or two would panic Caroline into selling to them, and then they could pull the whole thing down—get it listed as unsafe. It's been done before. All it needs is a greedy council official.'

'So that was that rumbling sound I heard the other night,' Jaime breathed, 'and your knuckles. . . .'

Blake caught the consternation in her voice and said coolly,

'The bulldozer driver came off much the worse of the pair of us—he was ten years older and running to fat. Strong enough to frighten a woman on her own, but something of a coward once he was removed from behind his machine.'

'Even so. . . .' She wanted to say that she had misjudged him dreadfully, and to beg his forgiveness, but how did one beg forgiveness for a sin, the enormity of which she was only just beginning to realise?

'Jaime, in view of all the publicity about this affair and the fact that Barrons are still bound to be feeling slightly raw, shall we say, I think it advisable for the three of us to go away—it won't seem too unexpected in view of all the circumstances. After all, we have just been reconciled.'

Jaime winced, wondering if she was being oversensitive to sense derision beneath the calmly spoken words.

'Away?'

'Yes.' Blake wasn't looking at her. 'A friend of mine owns a cottage in Pembroke. I've spoken to him by telephone and arranged to rent it from him for a couple of weeks. That should give all this fuss time to die down.'

'Pembroke,' Jaime stared at him with tear-sheened, disbelieving eyes, 'You mean the one where we spent our honeymoon?'

'You remember it?' Blake's eyes were hard. 'I am surprised. You left me with such unflattering alacrity, I'm also surprised to see how sentimentally it affects you.'

She wanted to cry out and scream, but her vocal chords were frozen in a paroxysm of pain. How could Blake do this to her?

He had left the room before she could object, coming back minutes later to add, 'We're leaving tomorrow. I've arranged to hire a saloon car. It will be more comfortable for the three of us than the Ferrari.'

'I'll need to go back to . . . to the cottage, to pack.'

'I'll drive you there on my way to pick up the hire car. Fern can come with me. . . . Unless, of course, you're still frightened that I intend to arrange her abduction.' He said it with such soft savagery that Jaime went white with the cruelty of the thrust.

'I'm sorry I misread the situation, but how was I to know any differently?'

'How indeed?' Blake's cold voice mocked her. 'Of course, it was only natural to assume that her father would lay her open to such danger; that indeed I should want to terrify and potentially injure you both. I suppose you even think I tampered with your brakes personally! Dear God, Jaime,' he burst out in a sudden explosive outburst, 'surely, you know I'd never. . . .'

'Not the car . . .' Jaime agreed in a stricken voice, 'but I think it was only meant to frighten me. If I hadn't had to brake for that child . . . and it was only threats where Fern was concerned . . . I just thought, when she went missing . . .' She swallowed hard, trying to control her shivering body.

'And yet you still let me make love to you,' Blake said softly.

'I. . . .' What on earth could she say to him, 'I couldn't help myself. I still love you . . .'? She shuddered, rejecting both explanations.

'No, don't tell me,' Blake intervened. 'I don't think I want to know.'

'Why did *you* make love to me?'

Jaime could hardly believe she had asked such a question. A curious expression crossed Blake's face.

'I don't think I can tell you the answer to that,' he said at last. 'It isn't very flattering to either of us.'

Hot colour scorched Jaime's face as he left the room. He meant that he had made love to her simply because she had been there, and she had not repudiated him, but, at least, he had not guessed her secret; he did not know that she still loved him.

Her mother expressed no surprise at learning they were going away. 'I think it's the best thing for all three of you,' she said calmly. 'You need time on your own as a family, and you're not likely to get it with everyone in the village wanting first-hand information about Blake's heroism.'

When Blake heard about the proposed dinner party he decided they would delay their departure until the Sunday.

'Good,' Jaime's mother pronounced when Jaime telephoned her with the news, 'That gives us time to go shopping on Saturday.'

'What on earth for?' Jaime asked her. 'I thought you bought plenty of new clothes before you went away.'

'I did,' she agreed, 'but you haven't. It seems to me that a second honeymoon, albeit with a small daughter in tow, calls for something a little more glamorous than the jeans and T-shirts that make up your wardrobe.'

'Pembroke is very quiet, Mother,' Jaime expostulated. 'We won't be dressing up to go out.'

'I wasn't thinking about when you go *out*,' her mother said mysteriously. 'I'll pick you up on Saturday morning. Blake can look after Fern.'

'Isn't it amazing how men change their minds about children once they arrive?' Sarah asked with a chuckle on Saturday morning as she and Jaime drove away from the Lodge. 'Fern can wind Blake round her little finger already.'

'Umm.' Jaime found she didn't want to talk about Blake's very obvious love for his daughter. She daren't allow herself to think about it because, if she did, she would have to face up to the problems there would be when she and Blake parted. In her eagerness not to spoil her mother's happiness she had completely overlooked the potentially devastating effects of her deception on Fern. Already, the little girl looked upon Blake as a permanent feature of her life. How would she feel when she realised that he wasn't?

'You're very gloomy.'

'Not really,' Jaime forced a smile and began to chatter enthusiastically about the coming holiday.

'Here we are,' Sarah parked deftly in front of a small shop Jaime had never noticed before. The window was decorated with a plain pink skirt and a toning silk-knit jumper.

'Italian,' her mother pronounced approvingly. 'This is my second time around wedding present to you, Jaime, so I'm going to choose.'

Half an hour later Jaime stood bemusedly by as her mother insisted on adding yet another pretty blouse to the pile of clothes already on the chair. There was a skirt like the one in the window, plus a jumper and several blouses; a pair of French-cut white trousers that flattered her slim figure; a soft, silky dress in pinks and lilacs, and, last of all, a whole set of delicate, shell-pink underwear, trimmed with écru lace.

'Oh no!' Jaime protested, 'They're far too expensive . . . and so delicate. I couldn't. . . .'

'You aren't doing,' her mother reminded her firmly, 'and I'm sure Blake will appreciate them even if you don't.' She and the owner of the small boutique exchanged grins while Jaime picked up the wispy briefs that tied in small bows over her hips. In addition, there was a bra, a camisole top and matching French knickers, a suspender belt, and an underskirt, as well as a frivolous, fragile silk teddy which the owner of the boutique suggested, without a blush, that she wore in bed rather than under her clothes.

'That's what the Americans do,' she informed them.

'Really? In my day, it was Chanel No 5,' Sarah announced irrepressibly. 'I used to fantasise about some gorgeous male buying me some— with the implied, but unspoken, desire that I should wear it in bed.'

As it was nearly lunchtime when they emerged from the shop, Jaime gave in to her mother's persuasion that they eat at a small wine bar in the centre of the town. On their way to it, they passed several shops, stopping to drool over shoes and matching bags in one of them.

'Jaime, just look at this,' her mother insisted. 'You must buy it—you can wear it tonight.'

'It' was the first of the new autumn fashions, a sapphire blue angora dress to match her eyes, with a tiny belted waist and a semi-circular skirt.

The dress had a boat neck and three-quarter sleeves, the back dipping in a low V.

'It's exactly the same colour as your eyes,' her mother pronounced. 'Let's go in.'

Although she had no intention of doing so, somehow Jaime found herself in a fitting room, trying on the dress. It fitted her perfectly, and she knew it suited her. The fine, soft wool hugged her breasts and narrow waist, the skirt emphasising the long length of legs. She knew she would have to buy it.

'Now, lunch, then we'll get you some shoes to match.'

Realising that her mother wasn't going to be swayed, Jaime gave in.

It was late afternoon before they got back to the Lodge. The saloon car Blake had hired stood outside in place of the Ferrari, and, as they drove up, Jaime saw Blake and Fern emerging from the drive that led to the Abbey.

'Everything's all right,' he told Jaime, when he saw her anxious face. 'I just wanted to have a word with the security guards.'

Jaime knew that two security guards now mounted a round-the-clock watch on the Abbey, and she wondered if Blake had engaged them on Caroline's behalf or if they were employed by the new owner-to-be. She hesitated about asking Blake any questions. He had become remote and withdrawn with her, only really behaving naturally when they were in the company of others.

Her mother refused her offer of a cup of tea,

explaining that she had to get back if she was to be ready in time for their meal.

'It's seven-thirty, don't forget!' she called out as she drove away, 'and don't forget to wear your new dress.'

Blake's eyebrows rose, but he made no comment. They might be living together, but there was no real communcation between them, Jaime thought despairingly.

Mrs Widdows was to have Fern for the evening. She would sleep in her old bedroom at the cottage, and they would pick her up on their way to Pembroke in the morning.

Blake made no comment when Jaime appeared in her new dress. She was also wearing her sapphire engagement ring, something she hadn't done all the time they had been apart.

'Still got that?' His eyebrows rose. 'I thought you must have got rid of it.'

'No.' The shocked denial was out before Jaime could silence it.

'Well, it can hardly have any sentimental value, unless it's to remind you of the disaster our marriage was,' Blake claimed acidly.

What could she say? That she had kept it because she loved him, and that she hadn't worn it because he hadn't loved her? All at once, her pleasure in her new outfit was gone. What had she expected, she wondered drearily? That a new dress would somehow make her irresistibly desirable in Blake's eyes?

'Daddy, you promised me a story,' Fern reminded Blake on their way to the cottage.

'And you'll get one, never fear,' he assured her, as they all got out of the car.

'You're going to have to watch it, Jaime,' Henry joked jovially, when they were all on their way out, Blake having come back downstairs with the news that Fern was fast asleep, 'otherwise, you might lose your husband to your daughter.'

Blake laughed, 'Yes, I confess I'm rather smitten with Fern.'

'What's the matter?' he asked, when he and Jaime were in his car. 'Are you jealous of Fern?'

'No, just surprised that you should admit you actually care about her,' she replied in a brittle voice. 'After all, you never *wanted* her.'

She saw his hands tighten on the steering wheel, and wished the bitter words unsaid.

'I didn't want us to have a child because I didn't think our marriage was stable enough to provide a secure home for one,' he bit out at last, 'and I was proved right. . . .'

'That's a lie,' Jaime threw back at him, her body and voice shaking. 'You didn't want a child because you didn't want to give up your precious freedom, your job ... even though you knew. . . .'

'My job was never the real issue between us, Jaime,' Blake said coldly. 'You just used it to mask your compulsive possessiveness and lack of self-esteem. If I didn't want us to have a child it was because I didn't think you wanted one for the right reasons.'

'No ... that's a lie. . . .' Jaime gasped out the words, but, in her heart of hearts, she knew they held some truth. When she first discovered she was having Fern, hadn't she thought that, at last, here was someone who was completely and absolutely dependent on her—that she would be the strong one, the dominant one in their relationship?

'Just as you wanted me to give up my job because you weren't mature enough to accept that being away from you didn't mean that I didn't care about you. I knew when I married you that you were immature, but I hoped that you'd grow. . . .'

'Into someone like Suzy?' Jaime bit out. 'How disappointed you must have been when I didn't. If you had wanted the sort of open marriage Suzy approves of, you should have married her, and not me. I can't imagine why you didn't. . . .'

'Don't be so childish. . . .'

They were within a mile of the restaurant where they were to eat. Jaime was close to tears of rage and humiliation. Somehow she had to get control of herself before her mother saw her.

'Whatever happened in the past is the past, Blake,' she said as evenly as she could. 'I don't deny that I was naive, and, yes, too clinging. I can understand how that must have irritated you, but you see it was because . . . I always knew you married me partially because you felt sorry for me, because I was so inexperienced, and I was so terrified of losing you.' There was a huge lump in her throat and nothing could have made her look at Blake, but she had to go on. 'Every time you left I was frightened that you wouldn't come back; that you would realise you had made a mistake in marrying me.' She couldn't go on. 'We're here.'

Henry's car turned into the car park ahead of them. There wasn't time to say any more, and Jaime was glad of the protective dusk when Blake opened the car door for her. She didn't want to spoil her mother's evening, so she talked gaily, avoiding Blake's eyes, hoping she was deceiving the others better than she was deceiving herself.

Blake was unusually morose, barely speaking to any of them. Surely, her mother and Henry must notice something, she thought nervously, but they were so wrapped up in one another and their love that they didn't.

'Why don't you two go and dance?' Sarah suggested, when she and Henry returned from the small dance floor.

'No. . . .' Jaime murmured her refusal, but Blake was already on his feet, his arm curving round her waist.

The tempo of the music slowed slightly as they reached the dance floor. Jaime tried to pull away as Blake circled her completely with his arms, but he wouldn't let her. Often, in the past, they had danced close together like this, but then she had leaned her head against Blake's shoulder, her palms pressed flat against his shirt front. Now, she tried to hold herself away stiffly, not wanting the torment of his body brushing hers, but he misunderstood her tension and said thickly, 'For Christ's sake, Jaime, I'm not going to rape you in the middle of a dance floor. Try to relax. We're supposed to be enjoying ourselves.' His hands pressed against her spine as he spoke, forcing her against his body. She could feel the heavy beat of his heart and smell his clean, fresh cologne. Her hands had nowhere to go, other than his chest. The dance seemed to last an unendurable age, but, at last, it was over. By the time they were ready to leave, Jaime's head was aching with tension.

Once they got back to the cottage, Henry insisted that they all have a nightcap. Fern hadn't stirred, Mrs Widdows assured Jaime. 'Don't worry about her. She'll sleep until morning,' her mother chimed in, 'and you'll be able to get ready much faster without her. She'll love the beaches. I remember the first time I took you to the seaside. You rushed on to the sand and started building a sandcastle.'

'She hasn't changed much, then,' Blake pronounced dryly, 'She did much the same thing on our honeymoon.'

And afterwards they had made love in the dunes, on the soft car rug Blake had spread there, watching the sea eat into her creation. All at once, she wanted to cry, but tears would change nothing, nothing at all.

CHAPTER TEN

JAIME's head was still aching the next morning from the tension, and wine, of the night before, when she and Blake drove to her mother's cottage in an uncommunicative silence. As she knew from their honeymoon, it was at least a four-hour drive to the Pembroke cottage, and she was glad when Fern fell asleep after the first hour.

'Another hour, and we'll stop somewhere for lunch,' Blake told her, but Jaime shook her head. 'Don't bother unless you're hungry. I'm not, and Fern will probably sleep through until we get there now.'

Apart from a brief tightening of his lips over her ungracious response, Blake said nothing.

The countryside flashed by them, Jaime trying not to remember how it had been the first time she had gone this way with Blake. They had just been married, and she had still been dizzy with wonder because he had wanted her. She stifled a small sound of pain, and tried to follow Fern's example, leaning back into her seat.

'Wake up, Jaime, we're here.'

Blake's voice sounded very close to her ear. Jaime reluctantly opened her eyes, appalled to discover that she was leaning against his shoulder.

'You've been asleep for ages, Mummy,' Fern

accused from the back seat, 'but Daddy said I wasn't to wake you.'

It must have been the tablet she had taken for her headache, Jaime thought muzzily, fighting against a reluctance to lift her head from its solid resting place. Poor Blake, his shoulder muscles must be quite stiff after supporting her weight for so long. If they were, he gave no sign of it, calmly reaching across her to release her seat belt, and then freeing his own before turning to free Fern from her seat.

For a man who had claimed that he never wanted children, he made a very caring father, Jaime thought as she opened her door and stepped out.

The cottage was miles from anywhere, perched on the cliffs with the National Trust pathway, that ran the whole length of the Pembrokeshire coast from St David's, only yards away from the front door. Small and compact, it had been an ideal honeymoon retreat, and Jaime knew that Fern would fall in love with the tiny, secluded beach within easy reach of the cottage, just as she had done.

The nearest village was three miles away and, during their honeymoon, Jaime and Blake had walked there when they wanted to reprovision. This time, she doubted that there would be long, private walks or lovemaking in the seclusion of the wild headllands. Not that they had spent all their time alone; they had gone one day to Milford Haven, to watch the naval vessels, and another to Haverford West. They had also visited

Pembroke Castle. Castles were something Pembroke was rich in, but Fern was too young to want to do much more than play on the beach.

The cottage was very much as Jaime remembered, with one double bedroom and the two smaller interconnecting ones, into which she put her and Fern's things.

'Would you like me to unpack for you?'

Blake was outside, still unloading the car, and he nodded his head briefly at her question. How polite and formal they were being to one another, and yet Jaime felt as though their politeness was unnatural, like the ominous silence before a thunderstorm. Only Fern seemed relaxed, chattering eagerly as she followed Jaime from room to room. The cottage had no television, and Jaime wondered how on earth she and Blake would pass the long, light summer evenings once Fern was in bed.

As Blake had told her, the freezer in the kitchen was well-stocked, and she had brought with her a selection of Fern's favourite foods.

After they had eaten, Fern insisted on going down to the beach.

'I'll take her,' Blake offered, and Jaime wondered, watching them go as she tidied up after their meal, if this resentment was something all women felt when they were excluded from the activities of their men and children.

Half an hour later they were back, Fern clutching some small shells, her face wreathed in smiles. They had paddled in the sea she told Jaime, as Jaime got her ready for bed, and then Daddy had climbed on some rocks. . . .

Telling herself that she was a coward, Jaime went downstairs and told Blake she was going to bed. 'I've had a headache all day,' she said, with some truth, 'and I think I'll have an early night.'

'I need to stretch my legs,' Blake informed her when she had finished, 'I'll lock up when I get back.'

Although she strained her ears, listening for sounds of his return, Jaime fell asleep before Blake came back, and their first evening at the cottage set the pattern for the evenings that followed.

The weather remained hot and sunny, but with a sultriness in the air that promised storms to come. Every morning Jaime took Fern down on the beach while Blake worked, using the portable typewriter he had brought with him. They returned at lunchtime when Jaime prepared a light lunch. After lunch, Fern napped while Jaime worked in the cottage garden or walked to the village.

Sometimes, later in the afternoon, they went out in the car, although these expeditions were seldom successful. Jaime felt that Blake was accompanying them as a duty, and his presence was a constant reminder of how much things had changed between them.

In the evenings he disappeared—to the village pub, Jaime suspected, where he, no doubt, found more congenial adult company than that to be had at the cottage.'

Their fifth day was much as the others, although it was hotter, the sky a brassy yellow colour. During the afternoon it became so sultry that it was as though the entire countryside was holding its breath.

Fern was in a fretful and irritable mood that ended in a temper tantrum and tears; for once, she seemed to prefer Jaime's company to Blake's, even to the extent of wanting her mother to read her bedtime story, something Blake had done ever since they had come to the cottage.

When Jaime finished settling Fern and went downstairs, she discovered that Blake had gone out. The thought of another solitary evening was just too much to be borne. A restless urgency pulsated through her body, but, of course, she could not go out and leave Fern.

Thunder rolled ominously in the distance, and there was no sign of Blake when Jaime went to bed. He would probably get soaked on the return journey from the village, because he had not taken the car. 'Serves him right for leaving me here alone,' she thought crossly.

Jaime was dreaming. She lay trapped in a cold, dark cave, with water dropping on her from the moist, unseen roof. She felt clammy and uncomfortable, but no matter how much she tried to wriggle away, the dripping continued. She shivered and woke up to discover that the dripping had been no dream and that her bedding was saturated from a leak in the ceiling above her bed.

Outside she could hear the fierce sounds of a storm, her curtains billowed at the open window, and the temperature had dropped several degrees. Cold and wet, she clambered out of bed in the dark, searching for the towelling robe she used for journeys to the bathroom, stubbing her toe on the base of the old-fashioned bed and knocking over a chair as she hopped up and down on one foot.

Lights sprang on outside her bedroom, the door opening as Blake strode in frowning, 'What the devil's going on?'

Like her, he was wearing a towelling robe, which he was hastily tying, as Jaime indicated the damp ceiling.

'There must be a slate loose. I'll get someone from the village to look at it tomorrow. It's probably been loosened by this storm. What about Fern's room?'

'I've only just woken up,' Jaime told him. 'I'll go and check.'

Fern was sleeping soundly and drily. Jaime turned back to her own room. Blake was leaning over the bed, pulling off the covers and the mattress which he propped up on its side away from the damp.

'What are you doing?' Jaime demanded.

'Propping this thing up so that we can get it dry. Tonight, you'll have to share with me. You can't sleep here,' he pointed out when Jaime was silent, 'and I'm certainly not giving up my bed to sleep on that apology for a settee downstairs. It's barely four feet long.'

It was, Jaime knew. Even she would be cramped up if she tried to sleep on it.

'I'll sleep in Fern's room—on the floor,' she said coolly.

'Don't be ridiculous,' Blake was frowning. 'Why make a martyr of yourself when there's a perfectly good double bed available—but then, you always did enjoy that particular role, didn't you, Jaime? Come on, leave this lot, we'll get it sorted out in the morning. You're cold,' he added, frowning when he saw her shiver.

'And wet,' Jaime agreed, shivering again. The thought of a cosy, warm bed was extremely alluring. She stifled a yawn. She really was too tired to argue with Blake tonight, and, after all, what was there to fear? That he might try to make love to her? 'Would that he would!' a small, inner voice sighed mournfully.

She looked for a dry nightdress, and then remembered that she had washed her spare one that morning and that it was downstairs in the ironing basket. She grimaced distastefully at the thought of keeping on the damp, clammy one she was wearing, and then remembered the silk 'teddy' her mother had bought for her. Eyeing it wryly, she took it with her into the bathroom. It was no more revealing than the cotton tops and shorts she had been wearing all week; but it was decidedly more provocative, she reflected, when she had towelled some warmth into her cold body and slipped it on.

During the week her skin had tanned, and it glowed softly beneath the fine fabric. The silk clung lovingly to her body, caressing it almost, but it was all she had to wear other than her undies, and so Jaime pulled on her towelling robe, and comforted herself with the thought that Blake would probably be asleep by now anyway.

He wasn't. He was propped up in bed, reading some typed sheets with the aid of a bedside lamp, when Jaime walked in.

Apart from glancing up when she opened the door, he paid no more attention to her. Even so, Jaime kept her back to him as she stood by her side of the bed and quickly slipped off her robe. That way, all he could see of her, if he did look, was her back. She sat down on the edge of the bed and pushed back the covers, and it was then, as she glanced up, that she saw the long pier mirror facing her. In it she could see both her own and Blake's reflection. He was leaning, watching her, his head propped up by one hand, his work forgotten, and Jaime's face flamed as she saw the *way* he was looking at her.

'If you've quite finished, I'd like to get some sleep,' she said icily.

'Why wear it if you didn't want me to see you in it?' Blake drawled easily. 'Why not stick to those cotton monstrosities you seem so fond of?'

'Because I only have two of them with me,' Jaime seethed. 'One is soaking wet, and the other is downstairs, unaired. It was either this or nothing. . . .'

'I think I'll go for the second option,' Blake said softly, and, before Jaime could stop him, Blake was reaching for the tiny pearl buttons that fastened the front of the teddy.

'Blake, stop it!' she lashed out at him with small, tight fists.

'Shussh. Don't make so much noise; you'll wake Fern,' he warned, ignoring her attempts to stop him, and easily imprisoning her wrists in the iron span of his fingers, securing them behind her back.

'Umm, very nice.' His free hand had worked the first few buttons open, and the silk fell away to reveal the tawny rise and fall of her breasts. Jaime kicked angrily out at him, quivering with anger. How dare he treat her like this! She had completely forgotten that, not ten minutes before, a part of her had longed for his lovemaking. The punishing grip of Blake's fingers jerked her wrists back so that she overbalanced, her arms still pinned beneath her by Blake's hand.

'Now what are you going to do?' he mocked softly. 'I know what I'm going to do, and it's this.'

'This' was his fingers flicking open the rest of the buttons that ran down to her navel. She looked like some slave girl spread out for her master's delectation, Jaime thought disgustedly, catching sight of herself in the mirror. Her skin glowed tawny against the soft silk, the rise and fall of her breasts tightening the frail fabric through which she could clearly see the outline of her own nipples. Even the way she had fallen on to the bed when Blake overpowered her suggested a sensuality that angered her, her body a languid sprawl of sleek, tanned legs and provocative, pale silk.

'Blake, this is ridiculous. Let me go at once,' she protested.

'In a moment. When you've told me you don't want me to do this . . .' He bent his head, and his tongue delicately flicked aside the fragile silk that covered one taut nipple, 'or this . . .' The tormentingly light, moist circles his tongue painted around her pulsating flesh had Jaime tensing her whole body against the urge to cry out the need his touch engendered.

'Well . . . tell me you don't, and I'll stop.'

She wanted to. Oh, how badly she wanted to, if only for the sake of her pride, but her tongue seemed to have stuck to the roof of her mouth. Speech was impossible. There was only feeling— wave upon wave of it—as Blake turned his attention to her other breast, repeating the torment he had already inflicted.

'You always did enjoy this,' he murmured shamingly, studying her flushed face with knowing eyes. 'You want to deny it, but you can't, can you Jaime? This,' he touched his mouth to the pulse pounding at the base of her throat, 'betrays you. It's no use, Jaime,' he told her softly, 'I mean to have the response from you I know your body wants to give, even if it takes all night.'

'Blake . . . please, you can't do this,' Jaime protested, making a last-ditch attempt to sway him. 'You can't use me, just to slake a sexual hunger. . . .'

'Why not?' he countered smoothly, with a barely discernible edge of anger under the soft words, '*You're* using me to protect your mother. . . .'

When he said that, Jaime knew she could not argue against him. Without another protest, she forced her body to relax.

'All right, Blake,' she said numbly, 'rape me, if you must, but just . . . just get it over with.'

'It won't be rape,' Blake told her softly, 'and I promise you, Jaime, you won't want me to "get it over with", but to prolong every tormenting moment of pleasure. You always did.'

It was useless to deny what he was saying. They both knew it was the truth. He bent his head, tracing a line of kisses down between her smooth breasts, down to where the final button lay close to her navel. Jaime drew in a sharp breath and then tried to release it as his tongue investigated the small hollow. She tried not to move but her body betrayed her, quivering in heated response to Blake's expert caresses. His tongue drew a line along the barrier of silk, and Jaime moaned protestingly, tugging her arms free. Blake released her, as though he knew that, this time, she didn't want to hold him off.

Her fingers stroked the smoothly compact muscles of his back, tracing the line of his spine, her body arching in helpless supplication to the sweet torment he was wreaking. When he lifted her hips to slide the silk free, Jaime sighed with pleasure, welcoming the sensation of skin against skin as the hard warmth of his thigh brushed against her. Now there was no question of her not wanting him to go on. Her whole body cried out for him, shamelessly telling him so, as it arched and seduced.

His mouth against her breast made her cry out with pleasure, her small teeth biting sharply into his skin.

'Jaime.' His hand rested possessively against her thigh, his voice commanding her to meet the hungry passion of his kiss. She gave herself up to it gladly, welcoming the hot invasion of his tongue, matching him in her need to convey her increasing need of him.

His fingers, caressing her intimately, transported her to a world she had nearly forgotten existed, her own hands reaching out to find the hard maleness of him.

Blake moaned his pleasure as her fingers stroked the throbbing tissue that told her of his desire, and Jaime knew that the moment of physical possession could not be delayed much longer, but she let Blake prolong the anticipation until it was almost a pain, kissing the moist warmth of his chest and then sucking the flat maleness of his nipples until his body shuddered in uncontrollable response, surging into hers with a fierce heat that satisfied the dull ache radiating from the inner core of her.

Their lovemaking was as fierce and elemental as the storm that raged outside, the powerful rhythm of Blake's body wringing from Jaime a shuddering response that made her cry out in a delirium only to find that, instead of reaching the peak of pleasure, they were still climbing; through the stars and into empty, dizzying space where Blake's mouth stifled her final cry of fulfilment, his tongue licking the tears of pleasure from her face.

Jaime fell asleep in his arms, her body still entwined with his, his arm a heavy weight against her.

When she woke up in the morning, Blake was gone. She could hear sounds of movement from downstairs, but, when she tried to get out of bed, she found her body lethargically uncooperative. She had just rescued the discarded teddy, when Fern burst into the room, closely followed by Blake.

'Breakfast,' he said calmly. 'I thought you might appreciate a lie-in this morning.'

Jaime could no more have prevented her brilliant flush than she could have flown. Blake's comment was as intimate as though he already knew of the love-bruises faintly colouring her skin and the pleasant ache still left in her body.

Half of her was relieved when he left her alone to eat her breakfast, and half of her disappointed. Where did they go from last night? Blake had never said he loved her, never mentioned permanency. . . . She would have to talk to him, Jaime thought despairingly. She couldn't go on sleeping with him, living with him, loving him as she did, while he . . .'

When she went downstairs, there was a note in the kitchen from Blake to say he had taken Fern down on to the beach.

The storm had left the air much clearer, and the sun shone out of a soft blue sky. Jaime brought the damp bedding downstairs and put it in the washing machine, only to discover that she was out of powder. The car was outside, and it wouldn't take her long to drive to the village. It took her longer than she thought to get back. The village shop was busy, and it was over half an hour before she could set off back.

As she drove up to the cottage, Blake rushed out, his face white and set.

'Jaime!'

'Fern?' she exclaimed anxiously, 'Has something happened to her?'

'Fern's upstairs having a nap. Where have you been?'

'To the village, to get some washing powder.'

Was it her imagination, or did Blake relax slightly?

'Where did you think I was?' she asked curiously.

'I thought you'd left,' Blake's voice was completely flat. 'Jaime, it's time we sat down and talked. I've tried to be patient, to tell myself to take it slowly, to give you time, but I just can't take it any more. I thought when you first left me that, if I gave you time, if I didn't frighten you, you'd stop hating me and start loving me again. . . .'

'Stop hating you?' Jaime stared at him, sinking down on to the wooden bench outside the cottage. 'But Blake, I've never hated you.'

'That's not what you told Suzy when you told her you were leaving me. "Tell him I hate him, and that if he tries to see me I'll kill myself"— that's what you told her.'

'No, I told her no such thing,' Jaime protested. 'She told me that you had asked to go on an assignment in El Salvador, that you were tired of me, that . . . Blake . . .'

He had dropped to the seat next to her, his head buried in his hands. 'Oh my God,' he said indistinctly. 'Is that really true?'

'Of course, it is. Why should I lie? I always loved you, Blake,' she said softly. 'Surely you knew that?'

'I knew you were infatuated with me. I knew I ought to give you more time to discover what life was all about. I knew I ought to give myself more time to accept that our marriage would mean a whole new way of life, but I also knew how desperately you craved security, and I was terrified that, if I didn't give it to you, someone else would. I told myself that, within the security of our marriage, you'd mature; that our love would mature, and that you'd stop being terrified of losing me . . . I was terrified that security was all you wanted from me, and that, one day, you'd grow up and realise that for yourself. . . . That's why I tried to get you to cling less . . . so that you could realise . . .' he shook his head. 'That day, when we had the quarrel, I'd already told them I wouldn't accept the El Salvador assignment. I knew I couldn't go and do the job properly, because too much of me would be left behind with you, but the moment I started to tell you about it, you threw that temper tantrum. . . .'

'Because I suspected I was having Fern, and I was so scared . . . so terrified that, once you knew, you'd be so angry that you'd leave. No children you had said. . . .'

'Because I wanted you to want them for the right reasons. Not because you needed someone to love. Dear God, Jaime! Of course, I wanted you to have my child.'

'So, why didn't you answer the letter I sent you telling you about Fern, and asking if I could come back?'

'You did that?' He looked distressed. 'Jaime, I left the flat the day after you. I was so bitter, so despairing that I told the editor I'd changed my mind, and that I would accept the El Salvador assignment. It was the last one I did accept. Suzy was the photographer assigned to me—we'd been lovers once, you know, not in the emotional sense, but merely in a physical one, and, while we were away, she made it plain that she wanted to resume our old relationship. I didn't— couldn't. I wanted only you, and, rather than embarrass her by telling her so, I decided to quit. I wanted to by then anyway. I'd always wanted to write. I got in touch with your mother the moment I got back, but she said she thought you wouldn't see me.'

Jaime remembered telling her mother, almost hysterically, how much she hated Blake. If she had told her the truth, how different things might have been!

'She advised me to bide my time . . . to wait . . . and I kept on waiting and waiting . . . and then she wrote to me and told me about Charles. I knew then I dared not wait any longer in case I lost you forever; so I decided it was time to re-enter your life.'

'Was that why you rented the Lodge?'

'Yes ... but nothing turned out the way I'd planned. Almost from the word "Go" I found that you and I had mysteriously got ourselves on the opposite sides of an argument. When I heard that Caroline was planning to sell the Abbey to Barrons, I was really worried. I knew all about their reputation, but I knew that if Caroline knew I was opposed to the sale. . . .'

'So you pretended to be in agreement with it?'

'I didn't want to be thrown out of the Lodge, I needed to be near you,' Blake told her. 'Jaime, about last night. . . .'

'It was one of the most beautiful experiences of my life . . .' Jaime said quietly, taking her courage in both hands. 'Blake, I've never stopped loving you, never stopped regretting leaving you, never stopped wishing I hadn't behaved so childishly. Every criticism you ever levelled at me was justified. I *was* immature, I *did* cling ... not because you offered me security, but because I couldn't understand what you saw in me. I could't believe you loved me. . . .'

'I told you you were short on faith and trust.'

'I thought you'd married me because you felt you had to—because I was a virgin,' she said simply.

She felt him draw in his breath and then release it, and then his hands were on her shoulders, turning her face to him.

'I married you because I loved you, because I

couldn't tolerate the thought of life without you, and then felt horribly guilty because I felt I'd used your inexperience to pressure you into a marriage you might later regret. We've both been guilty of confusing what is, basically, a very simple emotion, because, for different reasons, we couldn't bring ourselves to believe in it and one another.'

'Yes,' said Jaime sadly.

'I could wring Suzy's neck for lying to me, but I blame myself more. I should never have believed her, but you'd been so cold towards me those last few days. . . .'

'Because I suspected I might be pregnant, and I was trying to prepare myself for the loneliness I was convinced I would have to endure when you found out. I was sure you would leave me.'

'Never,' he averred softly. 'I still love you Jaime, and last night meant something very special to me, too. A chance to show you with my body, if I couldn't tell you the words, how much I still loved you.'

'And I love you. . . .'

'Which is just how it should be,' Blake grinned, teasing her, but there was nothing teasing in the warm pressure of his lips on hers, and Jaime responded to it joyously, letting the love she had struggled to conceal for so long show in her response.

'Now I know why you were so keen for us to come and live with you,' she smiled.

'Not entirely. I knew about Barrons' threats, and yet was powerless to do anything about them.

And there is one other complication you *don't* know about yet. You know the Abbey had another purchaser?'

Jaime nodded her head, puzzled.

'It's me,' Blake told her. 'I fell in love with it the moment I saw it. I couldn't help picturing you in every room, you and Fern, and the other children I wanted us to have, but I had to keep it a secret in case Barrons found out. The bulldozer episode was the the final clincher as far as Caroline was concerned. The very next day we signed contracts. If Barrons had known, they would have had even more reason to threaten you, Jaime. You'll never know how bitter I felt when I realised you thought I could harm so much as a hair on your head ... I wanted so much to tell you it all then ... but I was hurt, and I so wanted your love and your trust. . . .'

'So you deliberately and sadistically allowed me to go on thinking the worst,' Jaime said softly, remembering.

'It's all over now,' Blake drew her head down on to his shoulder, 'and, if you agree, we'll move into the Abbey just as soon as we can. I intend to go on writing and, athough there'll be some travel, you can always come with me.'

'I've grown up now, Blake,' Jaime said gently. 'I'm strong enough to trust. You see, all the time I knew I should suspect you I didn't, because, in my heart, I still loved you. . . .'

'Thank heavens for the leaking roof,' Blake murmured piously, just before he kissed her.

'Thank heavens indeed,' Jaime echoed

mentally, sliding her arms round him. From now on, there'd be no more separate beds, no more heartache or pain.

'Blake . . .' she began dreamily as his lips moved seductively over her face, 'how do you feel about a brother or sister for Fern?'

'Do you want me to tell you,' he asked wickedly, 'or show you?'